He Needed Killing

He Needed Killing

Book 1
in the
Needed Killing Series

Bill Fitts

He Needed Killing

Borgo Publishing Edition

ISBN 978-0-9883893-2-8

Cover design: Keri Knutson at Alchemy Book Covers

Printed in the United States of America

www.billfittsauthor.com

*For Anne, without whom
this book never would have been written*

CONTENTS

PROLOGUE

I was standing in a dead man's apartment staring at the severed end of a rope that was hanging from one of the exposed beams overhead. A good friend of mine, who happened to be the head of the Shelbyville homicide unit, was pointing at the rope, saying something about how the responding officers had cut it in hopes of reviving the deceased. Faint hope, of course, but they were trained to try.

What was I doing here? A week before, I was just a university retiree. A geek who had a geek's job before he'd decided the work wasn't worth the hassle and had taken early retirement. Now a man was dead, and somehow I was in the thick of it. People were counting on me to figure out what had happened— and why. What kind of retirement was this?

I got the news that he'd died and, after thanking Stan for calling, I hung up and stared at the phone. I shrugged my shoulders. It was just a fact. I couldn't summon up any feelings of sorrow or pleasure. As far as I was concerned he had needed killing. But dying of food poisoning at my retirement party? It seemed so trivial a cause of death for a man so despised. His victims deserved better. I walked out onto the screen porch and sat down staring out into the night.

Tan lifted up her head and cocked her ears forward, listening. She'd already been fed so she didn't bother to get up, but she was kind enough to show some interest. She wagged her tail, thumping it against the floor.

"Remember me talking about Idiot Boy? How I used to complain about him to you?" My dog isn't much of a conversationalist, but she listens and agrees with me. The cat, on the other hand, is just as likely to disagree as he is to agree.

"Turns out he died this afternoon. Food poisoning."

Tan put her head down and breathed a deep sigh. It was almost like she was relieved.

For a second I considered the futility of trying to explain food poisoning to a dog or a cat for that matter.

"Anyway, a few others were sick too, but nothing like Sean. Some of them didn't even go to the hospital."

Tan gave another deep sigh and I decided I was boring her. I picked up my glass and took a sip of scotch. I felt a little bad about it. After all, it was my retirement party. Not that I was there, you understand. I'd never intended to be there. But that's another story. It bothered me that a party ostensibly in my honor served food that made people sick—dead even.

Funny, I didn't even wonder what had made them sick. It had been so long since I'd gone to one of those things I wasn't even sure what was served. People usually suspected the mayonnaise—unjustly as it turns out. Mayonnaise actually prevents food from spoiling, commercial mayonnaise that is. You can make a pretty lethal homemade variety if the eggs are bad. But there I go again. Over the years I've accumulated a lot of bits of useful information. Either that or I'm a fount of useless information.

I felt the other half of my pet population bump my leg with his head. "So there you are. Did you hear the news?"

Soundlessly a large black cat appeared on the table; he was sleek and arrogant; he stared at me with intensely green eyes.

"It's true," I told The Black. "Stan's buddy at the hospital called him with confirmation. They're saying cause of death was food poisoning with complicating allergic reactions."

TB—short for The Black—just stared at me. Catlike, he was totally uninterested in the death of a man I'd hated. As far as The Black was concerned I should have fought it out with Sean tooth and claw just like he would have done. The nuances of human civilization are lost on TB. So too the fact that he's not supposed to be on the table. I picked him up and put him in my lap.

Tan and I had watched my retirement party proceedings, up to the point where Sean had collapsed, from the privacy of my pontoon boat—floating in the middle of the lake at a spot right in the line-of-sight of a wireless tower. I had gotten the wireless Internet card for the laptop just to see how well they worked. With a little testing I found that reception was best right where I thought it would be. It's nice when things work out that way.

The broadcast had worked just like Stan and I had planned. But I'm getting ahead of myself.

I had the time in to retire and the money—Eleanor's accident had seen to that. Heck, I'd been eligible for years, but I was having fun with what I was doing. So why retire? Then Sean came in and took over the Department of Technology. And that changed everything. I could go into detail, but let's just say it wasn't fun any more. So I decided to retire.

It turns out that in the real world deciding to retire is one thing and actually retiring is quite another. I should have expected it. The state retirement system is an entirely separate entity from the university. And each had its own set of rules and regulations. That was bad enough but the state legislators would periodically pass some silly piece of legislation to keep state employees from benefiting from being employed by the state. State university, state retirement system, state legislators—I shouldn't have been surprised.

Still, for reasons passing my understanding, I couldn't just pick a day and stop coming to work. When I suggested to my retirement counselor that it seemed to me to be the easiest way to handle it she had reacted in horror. It was explained to me that "no, no, that's not how it's done." I had to leave at the end of a pay period so that I could be shifted from the active to the retired group and keep my eligibility for this and that, not disrupt coverages, and match up with fiscal accounting periods. I finally gave up trying to make sense of it and let the system determine what my retirement date was going to be. Once the system had determined the date of my official last day of work, I had smiled politely, notified my department, cleaned out my office, and stopped going to work. I had plenty of vacation time accrued and saw no reason why my last day of work couldn't be a vacation day. I had no intention of working for the university any longer.

Some of the administrative types had a problem with my approach but what were they going to do?

Then there was the issue of the retirement party.

Whenever an old-timer leaves the university, his department throws him a retirement party. At least they do at this university. Maybe it's a southern university thing. I wouldn't know. Anyway, it doesn't matter if everybody is glad or sad to see the person go. They have a party where people stand around and tell stories about the old days—some real, some imagined. For salaried employees, it's always on the last workday of the month and in the afternoon. Anyway, at the proper moment, the retiree's boss tells a funny story involving the retiree-to-be, says a few pertinent words, and then wishes him or her well followed by a general round of applause. The retiree, in turn, acknowledges the kind words and good wishes, tells everyone that it will be the people they'll miss, not the place, and thanks everyone. It's all pretty well scripted.

I wasn't interested in a party—not on that date and not under those circumstances. Sean, on the other hand, took it as a personal affront that I would deny him an opportunity to wish me well in retirement. The cynical might say he wanted to gloat about having driven me to retirement and that might have been a part of it, but I think the reality was that he loved to hear himself talk. He hated being denied an opportunity, particularly in front of a captive audience.

So much for the wishes of the guest of honor. Sean wanted me to have a retirement party and, by god, I got one. And it killed him. I shrugged and felt my lips twitch into the beginnings of a smile. OK, so maybe there was a little humor in the great

Sean Thomas being laid low by mayonnaise or whatever was the real culprit.

Sean had determined that the party would be held in the open area outside his office. What he liked to call the "campus." He had created the space by moving employees into cubicles and destroying their old offices. It was sort of like urban renewal. The fact that I was not going to be in attendance might have argued for a smaller venue, but Sean had spoken. That way he could stand in the doorway to his office and smile benevolently on the peons that milled before him. And spot anybody important enough to invite into his office for a quick chat.

Because people from all over campus would come. Some to assure themselves that I was gone, others to mourn the passing of an era. I'm not being immodest, it's the truth. I had been too much of a maverick and the university too small a town, if you will, to spend thirty-five years in it and not be well known—or infamous I suppose.

Food would be packed onto the conference table with nuts and chips to munch on scattered around the area. The one sure way to get geeks to come to these things was to offer them food. Drink would have worked too, but the university had an official policy against serving alcohol at business functions. (Tell that to the athletic booster club!) There would be a punch bowl but whatever was in it would have no kick.

Sean had his event coordinator roll out the appetizers, cold meats, salads, and a retirement cake. In the old days everyone would have been encouraged to bring a dish from home so there was more of a personal flavor to the events. Somebody was famous for their parmesan cheese and onion dip, someone else for fried rice, seven-layer dip, sausage balls, cheese straws, and so on—staples that would be at everybody's retirement party until the person who made the dish retired. But Sean had put an end to that. He preferred to use a caterer. The university's Food Services department, I admit, but outsiders anyway. It was another way Sean had found to strip the department of any remnant of the culture that had existed before he arrived. His scorched earth approach extended even to catered events.

Hmmm, I'd forgotten about that. So the food had been professionally prepared. That made his death even more ironic. I allowed myself a small smile.

Anyway, the people who wanted to eat came at the appointed hour, as well as those who wouldn't miss an event just so they could say they had been there. And almost everybody else who worked for Sean, or worked for people who worked for him. A few of the people I had worked closely with didn't want to attend, but the word had come down. Sean was giving a speech and he wanted an audience. Oh, and don't think anyone's absence wouldn't be noted. So the ones who were afraid of Sean, they came. And the ones who told themselves that they weren't afraid, just cautious, they came too.

Peggy Franklin was there, poor soul, because she had to be. When she had asked me about a retirement party, I had told her I didn't want one, wouldn't go to one, and would refuse to acknowledge anything that came out of it. She knew I meant it and still she had to plan the party.

Peggy had two more years before she could retire. And Sean was making those two years look more like twenty. He called her his administrative assistant and thought that made it all right to then have her drive him around campus in her own car or fetch his tea when he couldn't be bothered and then complain about how she'd made it too hot. Veronica Anson and Albert Worthy were there too—his toadies. The former was his fiancée and the latter his deputy chief of operations. Officially she was in charge of special projects for the controller, but that was part of the deal, read "employment package," that brought Sean to our fair campus. The whole Department of Technology leadership committee (their description, not mine) was there; they'd have been fools not to be. And they weren't fools exactly. Oh well, let's get back to the party.

Since I wasn't there to hear the tributes and tales of my behavior and nobody but Stan knew the party was being streamed over the Internet, there didn't seem to be much reason for Sean to give a speech. It's not that I'd worked for him long enough to have a history. He certainly didn't want to repeat any of our private conversations. But the invitations had said that the great man would be making some remarks and no one wanted to leave before they heard what those remarks were going to be. So people mingled while they waited, some swapping tales among themselves, keeping their voices down as they said to one another, "Old Crawford did this, or said this, or I'll never forget the time . . ." But most smiled nervously at one another and said as little as possible as they substituted food for conversation. It was standing room only around the conference table/buffet table.

Sean was standing in his office doorway. When he judged the time was right, he cleared his throat and glanced at Albert, giving him a nod.

"Sean," Albert's voice was deeper than you'd have thought, "don't you think you should go ahead and say a few words about Crawford? We could record it and send it to him."

"Can you set that up?" Sean thoughtfully rubbed his chin as if they hadn't already rehearsed it. "Kind of appropriate to send the premier audiovisual man a recording of his retirement party. I like it," a forceful nod. "Let's do it."

We'd set the area up for monitoring before I left. Over the years I had been involved with most of the university's surveillance wiring. So it should have worked a treat, but I'm getting ahead of myself.

Albert glanced over to Stan Dowdy and Paul Simms, Stan's student worker. "You can set that up, right?" They nodded in unison not daring to look at one another for fear of bursting out laughing. Stan ran his right hand through the short stubble he called a haircut, "I think I can do it from here." He pulled out his cell phone and ran his finger across its smooth surface.

"Oh," said Albert, "is there an app for that?"

Stan looked up. The cameras and microphones were live and had been for an hour or two. One thing you learned in our business is that it's the shot you missed that you wished you had. That was when you used film. Nowadays it's disk space. And we had plenty of disk space. "An app?" he looked down at his phone his smile hidden. "Sort of. Yes, it's rolling," He gave Albert the thumbs up.

Albert nodded. "All right, let's do it. Go ahead, Sean."

Then the great man picked up a coffee mug that was sitting on a small table near the door to his office, took a big swallow, put it down, patted his stomach, and stepped out of his doorway. "Unaccustomed, as I am to public speaking," he stopped, coughing into his fist as the audience chuckled, "I would like to make a few comments about our ex-coworker James Crawford." He paused and rubbed his stomach again. A look of concern crossed his face. "I'd like," Sean hunched over and gripped his stomach. He made a garbled sound, vomited, and crumpled to the carpet. (The carpet, by the way, was new and very ugly.) There was a sudden silence as everyone took a breath.

"Sean?" exclaimed Veronica her voice high and thin. "What's wrong?" She crossed the room to kneel beside the body. Sean had vomited again and then curled up into the fetal position.

Don Larson, head of security, squatted down on the other side of the body. "Looks like food poisoning and it has hit him hard. He's lost consciousness." Don looked up at the circle of people standing around staring wide-eyed. "Peggy, call 911 and get an ambulance here right away! The rest of you step back, people, and give him some air. And for god's sake, everybody stop eating the food!"

Veronica, as usual, challenged Don's knowledge and instructions. After all, he only had a bachelor's degree. "Food poisoning? Was it the potato salad? Sean's allergic to potato salad. But how would you know? We need a doctor!" She ended with "get somebody who knows what they're doing in here," before subsiding into sobs.

Don stood up during her outburst. "I was a medic in the army, not that it matters. I've seen some problems with food— here and overseas." He pointed at Sean who had started to groan, obviously in pain. "It looks like it to me—symptoms are the same. A damn severe case, I'll give you. Did you say he was allergic to something?"

Veronica just stared at him.

"When he gets to the hospital that's one of the first things they are going to ask—right after whether he's insured."

. . .

Sean's "campus" area had been wired for sound and video. Directional mikes and movement-activated or remote-controllable cameras along with the standard fixed devices. All piped across the Internet. The party had been streamed in real time. It was a neat accomplishment. The website was basically a page of thumbnail pictures. Click on one and you could zoom in with a remote-control camera. Click on another and you'd have a different point of view. As you switched between them, you could mute sounds or increase the audio sensitivity. Or open up another window. A nice piece of work we'd done. As it turned out, a very nice piece of work.

What we had done was to monitor the "campus" with cutting-edge technology and state-of-the-art equipment. Once we'd done all that, the equipment pretty much sat idle. When we decided on our own to make the party visible to anybody who had an Internet connection and knew where to look, we built the website. So someone could see the party they didn't want to go to. One of the cameras had gone bad so there was just a thumbnail of a gray screen where its feed should have been.

Did you know that a laptop with a wireless access card can get a nice wireless connection out on the lake? Clear line of sight to a relay tower. It's probably not common knowledge, but I like to "investigate new technology." I think that's a nicer way of describing it than "I like to play with expensive toys."

I admit there's no difference, it just sounds better.

But that's how I was able to watch my retirement party and see Dr. Thomas collapse from food poisoning. That's why Stan had called. He knew I'd seen Sean collapse but I had no way of knowing that he'd died or that others had been taken ill.

CHAPTER 2
THURSDAY MORNING

"Is that what you're wearing these days? What do you call them? Retirement clothes?" Captain Jim Ward, one of Shelbyville's finest, and head of the homicide unit, had ignored the front door, walked around the house, through the gate into the backyard, to find me sitting on the screen porch drinking coffee and staring at the backyard. It's not an unusual place for me to be so he'd found me there before. My dog, Tan, as usual, had barked wildly at Jim, all the while wagging her tail and waiting to be petted. She rarely barked at strangers. I think she waited to see if I was going to bark at them—leader of the pack stuff.

I glanced down at my sweat-stained T-shirt and shorts and then looked at Jim's suit and tie. "I'm more comfortable than you are," I sneered. "Look at you wearing that monkey suit."

"Monkey suits, I believe, are technically tuxedos." He stepped up to the table and hooked one of the chairs with his foot, dragging it out in front of him. "Mind if I sit? I have to ask since you seem to have lost your manners. As far as comfort goes, I'm much more comfortable in this when I'm working than in clothes like yours."

I knew once I'd said it that monkey suits was the wrong expression so I glared up at him. And felt my neck tighten. He was over six and a half feet tall and liked to take advantage of it. It was a good technique, to make the suspects feel small and threatened. I'd have used it if I were in his line of business. And had his height.

"Well, I'm not working except in the yard later, which," I looked down at my old sneakers, "explains why I'm dressed the way I am. Not that it matters." I nodded at the chair, "Take a load off your feet. Coffee?"

"Wait a minute," Jim stepped back. "Let's not forget that I am working. Don't think plying me with good coffee will keep me from my duty to bring all miscreants to justice!"

I got up and went into the den. If the weather was good I left the door open between the screen porch and the rest of the house. Sometimes during storms I left it open just for the sounds and smells. The dog and cat didn't much care for that during storms. The den led into the kitchen. I grabbed a mug and put it on the window sill. The prior owners had added the porch across the back of the house. The window over the kitchen sink now opened into the porch. I usually left that open too. I had a thermos of coffee, half-and-half, and sweetener out there already.

Jim picked up the mug and turned back to the table.

"Yeah, well if I ever commit a murder I won't expect any favors. What about parking tickets?"

"Hell, Crawford," growled Jim. He sat and reached for the thermos. "I can't do anything about university parking tickets. Besides if you'd park where you're supposed to park you wouldn't get tickets." He poured himself some coffee, added half-and-half, stirred, and sipped. "Or, by chance, are you trying to get me to help you with one issued by a member of the Shelbyville police?" His eyes peered at me over the cup, his voice deepened. "Pay the ticket. We need the money."

"Spoken like a true defender of truth, justice, and the American way." I toasted him with my coffee cup. "So to what do I owe this visit? Office coffee machine broken again?

"Good coffee," said Jim, "what is it?"

"French roast, fair trade." It was good coffee. I bought it whole bean instead of ground. My coffeemaker ground the beans as part of making coffee. One of the ways I indulged myself.

"Oh, just checking in on you. Heard about your retirement party and wondered how you were bearing up."

"Retirement party?" I reached for the thermos to top off my cup and Jim pushed it to me. "I'm doing OK. I didn't go to it—those that did—well." The thought struck me. "You investigating it? Sean's death that is, not my retirement." I took a sip of coffee, pleased at how well the thermos held the heat.

Jim shook his head. "Food poisoning? Nope. Oh, we started to look into it until we got the emergency room doctors saying the victim had food allergies. That was just before the ambulances started arriving with the people from that pile-up. Why do people think just because the car in front of you made it through the intersection you can too?" He shrugged his shoulders. "I guess it's the same kind of thinking as deciding you can go on green without looking.

"But to answer your question, things aren't so slow that I go looking for work. Unless you think it was murder. I know you didn't think much of the deceased."

"No, I think if anybody at work had decided to kill him they'd have gone right after him and not depended on poisoning the food. That might have killed people other than Sean. As it was, other people got sick. Sloppy." I read murder mysteries and over the years I've developed an attitude about how it's done. It's provided Captain Ward with great entertainment—once or twice bringing him almost to tears.

"There you go with your idealistic ideas about murderers!" Jim chuckled to himself. "As if they cared about innocent bystanders.

I frowned. "I'm not sure you can call it idealistic."

"Right! I should have said unrealistic."

We'd had these discussions—half-arguing, half-joking—over the years. In a nutshell it all came down to the fact that I believed the murderers Jim dealt with year in and year out just weren't the kind that you'd write a book about. At least a book that I'd want to read. On the other hand, Jim was so conditioned to suspect the spouse, family, and random acts of violence that he'd never detect a murderer who wasn't an obvious suspect or a death that wasn't clearly a murder.

"Sloppy?" Jim grinned widely. "The sloppiness was in the food preparation and I don't think any district attorney's going to think that somebody not washing their hands was the equivalent of premeditation." He lifted the cup of coffee to his lips.

I stopped, my coffee cup halfway to my lips. "Do you suppose that's what happened? Somebody killed Sean and tried to cover it up with food poisoning?"

My timing had been perfect. Coffee exploded out of Jim's mouth as he tried to contain himself. "Spit-take," I handed him a napkin, "highest compliment you can give a joke."

"I'm glad you think it's a joke." He wiped his sleeve and then the table. "I'd have a hell of a time convincing my boss that a death from food poisoning was worth investigating."

I raised an eyebrow, questioningly.

"Don't you read the papers? The state's slashing everybody's budget for the third year in a row. Not a time to be spending time and money on proving an accident was an accident."

"What about that 'truth, justice, and the American way?' I mentioned earlier?"

"Superman wasn't on the payroll, eligible for benefits, or in the pension plan."

I nodded. I'm pretty sure the average citizen had no idea what the budget cuts were doing to law enforcement and I was pretty sure that the powers-that-be didn't want them to begin to suspect. Since they weren't going to get the money anyway, why scare the public?

"It was probably a food allergy. I think I heard Voni say he was allergic to potato salad or some such after he collapsed." I waited wondering if Jim was going to ask.

"Yeah, food allergies could explain why one person died while the others had mild reactions—mild compared to death that is." He paused then looked at me. "Heard—at the retirement party? How so? Aren't you the man that wasn't there?"

. . .

So I described to him the layout of Sean's campus—an open space he'd created by tearing down offices and how I'd wired it with cameras and microphones so that everything that happened there could be captured and broadcast over the Internet— everything, well—everything except what it smelled like. If we'd been able to capture smells we might be able to tell what dish had spoiled.

I was waxing eloquent about the advantages of one microphone over another when I noticed Jim glancing at his wristwatch. I'd done it again—sometimes I get carried away with my gadgets. "But I bet you need to get back to work—not listen to a retiree filling up his day with talk."

Jim grinned. "Oh, it was interesting listening to whatever it was you were talking about. I was wondering how you were dealing with retirement. By the way, when were you going to mention the fact that you had retired to me? Or were you going to send out announcements after the party?"

Damn. I had forgotten to tell him. Who else have I forgotten to tell? Forgotten? Hell, I hadn't even thought to let people know.

"It's not that big a deal. Retirement that is. Technically I've retired from working at the university." I shrugged. "Besides, I didn't want a retirement party even before Sean Thomas came to Shelbyville, Jim. I've told you that."

"Got no problem with that." He eyed me appraisingly. "It was the fact that you hadn't talked about it—to me and some others I talked to. But Stan tells me that most of the university people knew about it. Of course you didn't give them a list of whom to tell, so some people might not have gotten the word. As far as Stan knew nobody had told people in town about it."

"You talked to Stan about me?"

"Sure enough." Jim stood up. "Wanted to make sure you weren't digging a hole and hiding in it like you did before. He eyed me carefully. "It was five years ago yesterday, wasn't it—the day Eleanor died?" He picked up his coffee cup, put it on the window sill, patted Tan on the head, and pushed the door into the yard open. "Interesting that you'd pick the anniversary of her death as the day to retire. Call me if you want to talk." He turned around and headed for the gate.

. . .

After Jim left, I sat with my feet propped up on the table, heels together, toes apart, staring at nothing through the vee my shoes made. I was trying to think.

Trying to think about what Jim had said. It wasn't real pleasant. I felt like I'd let him down—him and all the others I hadn't
told that I was going to retire. Looking back—I find my hindsight a hell of a lot more accurate than my foresight. Looking
back, I can see how what seemed like a reasoned, logical, and
rational decision-making process to me might look from the outside like I woke up one morning, went to work, announced my
retirement, and left. How many others had noted that my official
retirement date was the anniversary of Eleanor's death?

For the first time in a long time, I wondered what Eleanor
would have said. She had always been more sensitive to the feelings of others. I nodded to myself. Yeah, maybe I should have
made the rounds saying good-bye to those who deserved it. I
wasn't having a retirement party, so I should have gone to them.
Courtesy.

. . .

The computer center must have resembled an anthill that had
been run over by a lawnmower. The whole top of the hill disap-
pears. You look down and, at first, there's no sign of life. Then,
suddenly, ants are swarming all over the place. Sean's sudden
death must have created chaos in the department—an instant
power struggle caused by the vacuum at the top. Work has to go
on, but who decides what gets done? The leadership committee
can't meet because no one but Sean had the authority to call a
meeting. Albert, the deputy director, would be trying to coordinate things, but without Sean's backing he'd be having a hard
time getting people to pay attention. Sean had used fear to manage people. With him gone . . .

And that was just within the department. All over the university, users would be calling to find out what had happened and to find out why their problems hadn't been solved. Or to report new ones. And as the news spread across the campus? And on to other academic settings? It would be a wonder if anything got done.

Except football, of course. This being the start of the fall term, football would take precedence. Too bad it hadn't happened during the summer. Things were slower during the summer and that meant things got a closer look. It took until the next week before I began to suspect that maybe Sean's death was related to the football season.

. . .

I glanced around, looking at the projects I had on hand and those were just the ones in the backyard. Projects I was going to get to now that I had retired. A bunch of them were just maintenance; others had been "in the works" for who knows how long. Some of them Eleanor and I had talked about doing years ago. Sometimes I'd take something off the list and end up doing it anyway.

What time was it? I Looked at my wrist and was surprised to see that there was no watch on it. The tan line had faded away since I had seen no need to wear a watch once I retired. I reached for my cell phone, checked the time, put it down, and realized I'd forgotten what it said.

Sean's death must have shocked me more than I had realized. It wasn't that I was grieved by the loss. After all, to me, as we say around here, Sean was a man who needed killing. And I wasn't the only one to think so.

I needed people around me. People to talk to—people to listen to. Face-to-face conversation—phone calls wouldn't do.

I stood up, walked to the door, and spit on the ground. "Needed killing," I muttered to myself, turned around and walked into the house. To the shower, shampoo, razor, and all the rest that followed. I had decided. I was going into work. Of course, I didn't work there anymore, but I knew what I meant.

CHAPTER 3
LATER THURSDAY MORNING

Stan looked up from his monitor and turned to see who was behind him. That would be me.

"I will be dipped in shit," he exclaimed half under his breath, then jumped to his feet. He put out his hand for me to shake. "Ford, I thought you were never going to darken my doorway again!" He was quoting somebody. Me, of course.

I shook his hand. He must have been surprised. Stan never cursed. It just wasn't his way. "Your office doorway," I corrected. "And we should know better than to say never. At least I should know better even if you don't. Still sitting with your back to the door." I shook my head. "Bad habit."

"Like I haven't heard that before." Stan pointed to a chair. "Sit. Old guys like you need their rest."

"Didn't think to call and say I'd be coming in. Sorry."

Stan sat and leaned back. A smile slowly spread across his broad face. "Well, I'm guessing that even you couldn't stand it." He nodded. "You just had to come in to make sure you hadn't dreamed it. Sean's death, that is."

I nodded, "Yes, that's part of it. In addition, Captain Ward came out to the house this morning. Said he'd talked to you."

"Yeah, he talked to me when he came out to check out the campus." Stan pointed up at the ceiling. His office was directly below Sean's. "Seems like you didn't tell him you were retiring."

I grimaced. "He mentioned that to me." I paused. "And I guess I should have. On the other hand he didn't mention he'd been here to me. Was he investigating Sean's death?"

"Yeah, guess the homicide squad checks into these things to some extent when anybody dies. Just in case it was murder." Stan chuckled. "If it had been murder, I'd have put you at the top of the suspect list myself." He shook his head, "No, I take it back. Why would you waste your time on him? You're retired. Why kill him now?"

"Right," I said. "Glad to see you understand. Does anybody really think it was more than food poisoning?"

"Of course we do, because we all know you wanted him dead." I recognized the voice coming from the doorway. "And for you to kill him at your retirement party? A party that there was no chance in hell of you attending? Sweet, Crawford, very sweet. A built-in alibi. And just like you."

"Thanks, Bobby." I grinned at the small woman who stood in the doorway. Her hair had gone gray early and, after a few rounds with different colors, she and it had reconciled. Now few knew if her age had caught up with her hair color. "It's that kind of comment that makes the police department waste the taxpayers' money looking into a simple food allergy. Keep it up and I'll end up getting taken," I dropped my voice, "downtown for questioning." I smiled at her. "What brings you to the computer center? Misery looking for company?"

"I didn't say you were the only person who wanted him dead. Lots of others would get taken," she dropped her voice as well, "downtown for questioning." Her smile could brighten up any room. Sometimes it was blinding, just depended on the wattage. "Hell, he's not the only person on campus who needed killing. The press has its own candidate, as you well know."

"Whew, there for a second, Bobby, I thought you were talking about me," said Stan. "And I know why you're standing outside my door. You figure emails and phone calls haven't gotten you that video clip I promised you and now you've come to drag it out of me. Sorry!"

"What!" I exclaimed in mock dismay. "Stan missing a deadline! Is the world coming to an end? That's as hard to believe as Bobby missing one."

"And the only reason I'm 'standing outside' is this jerk who doesn't know to stand up and offer a lady his chair."

"I believe," I said as I stood up, "that I have much to learn about being retired. The first thing, obviously, is not to get in the way of those who are working. My apologies to all." I bowed at Bobby and with a flourish held the chair out for her to sit on. "Please, my lady, take my seat. Retiree that I am, I've come for the gossip. Tell me, what say the jungle drums?"

As Bobby sat she and Stan exchanged questioning glances. "Well, I heard it was the potato salad," said Bobby, "is that what you mean? That's the word sweeping the campus. I think even the student newspaper is reporting it that way." She stopped and looked puzzled. "Considering how rarely the paper gets the facts right, one could make the argument that potato salad can't be the answer."

All three of us smiled at the legendary ability of student reporters to report the exact opposite of what actually happened.

"That's what made everybody else sick—as far as we've been able to tell." Stan shrugged his shoulders. "Everybody who got sick remembers having some but there's no way of determining exactly what caused it."

"Why is that?" Bobby looked puzzled. "Did they eat all of it?"

"No. Food Services got rid of all the evidence before we knew Sean was dead. It was gone before the police got here."

"Captain Ward must have loved that." I threw in my two cents' worth.

"Well, nobody told them not to clean up and after Sean collapsed and the others got sick the party was definitely over. So they cleaned up." Stan crossed his hands over his ample paunch. "I'd have gotten rid of the food too, if I'd been in Food Services. Can you imagine the lawsuits?"

I shrugged my shoulders and threw my hands up in mock despair. "Destruction of evidence! It's a good thing he wasn't murdered. But why did he have to eat tainted potato salad at my retirement party? For that matter, how much potato salad did he eat? Two or three times what the others did?"

"Who knows? I thought somebody said something about a food allergy. Maybe it didn't matter how much of it he ate."

"Just think," said Bobby, "what if he'd waited until next weekend to nibble on some potato salad—if that's what it was? He could have died at his wedding reception. What a mess that would have been—for the groom to die right after getting married."

"Wedding? Next weekend?" I was confused.

"That's right, you probably didn't hear about it." Stan glanced at Bobby. "I'm surprised the news got to the Press that quickly."

Bobby smiled. "The director got an invitation and asked who 'this Sean Thomas' was. Stands to reason he wouldn't have any idea who was in charge in technology."

Stan nodded. "And that Sean would have invited everybody at the university who was director level or higher."

"Is this that on-again, off-again marriage to Veronica Anson?" I was beginning to catch on.

"That's right. But this time it was on—on with a vengeance. A couple of weeks ago Sean took a look at the football schedule and discovered next weekend was the last away game until late September. He jumped on it. There was no chance of any more postponements. They were scrambling to get things lined up."

"Still," I commented, "who serves potato salad at a wedding reception?"

"The same people who serve it at a retirement party. Who do you think was doing the catering?"

"Food Services? The people who run the university's cafeterias?"

"Right." said Stan. "The very same. Limited menu, I'm told."

"They were lucky to get Food Services, limited menu or not," added Bobby. "You know how everything has to be scheduled to avoid conflicting with home games. I doubt if there was a caterer in town who wasn't already booked."

"What was the rush?" I asked. "Shotgun wedding?"

"The Ice Queen?" Stan laughed. "That doesn't seem likely to me. Never did understand what he saw in her. As far as I know it was just one of Sean's things. You remember. He'd make a decision and we'd have to kill ourselves getting it done."

"Maybe she told him she was tired of waiting?" Bobby glanced at me and then Stan. "How many years has she been the future Mrs. Thomas? Weren't they engaged when they came here?"

Stan shook his finger in a mock scold. "Now, Bobby, you know she's got her doctorate. It was going to be Doctor and Doctor Thomas. She wouldn't have it any other way."

"Come to think of it," I put it that way since I had, indeed, just thought of it, "I wonder how lucky they feel now about their choice of caterer? Well, how lucky Voni feels. Sean is beyond feeling."

Stan leaned forward to look down the hall making sure no one could overhear him. "She's holding up right well, I'd say. She came to work—been acting like she was appointed interim director."

There was silence while we each considered that tidbit of information.

"Ice Queen," repeated Stan.

"Ouch," added Bobby in a whisper.

. . .

I changed the subject. No use dwelling on the fact she was at work. "But that's not why I came in today."

"Well, I can tell it wasn't to see me because I'm not usually here." Bobby smiled. "I'm hurt, come to think of it, that you didn't just come over to the Press building—if you even know where it is."

I thought about it for a second. "Actually, now that you mention it, I have never been in your building—I've only got a general idea where it is. Why is that?"

"Because all of us who work there would rather meet somewhere else. Anything to get away from Philip Douglas—the biggest jerk on campus."

I grinned. "Maybe he is—now that Sean is dead. Don't know if he could have claimed that title before now. But you're right, I did come by to see Stan. It seems that yesterday an event was held on campus that was captured on camera and streamed over the Internet without anyone's knowledge or consent. It's one thing to just stream it live, but it might have been recorded. Recording without consent is a different ball of wax. People responsible for things like that can get in trouble, you know." I was carefully not looking at Stan.

"And some of it even was streamed out to the middle of Lake Shelby."

Out of the corner of my eye I saw Bobby open her mouth to speak and stop, eyes cutting back and forth between the two of us.

"Some of it was streamed over the Internet," said Stan. "When you stream video like that you can't aim it."

"Point taken." I paused. "But what did get out on the Internet wasn't everything that was captured. Not everything the cameras saw." I interrupted myself. "What's with the one that stopped working anyway?"

"Peggy cut the power line. You know that little whine they make when focusing?"

"Yeah, what of it?"

"It was the one near her 'station.' What we used to call desks. The noise was driving her buggy." He shrugged his shoulders. "I figured she had it bad enough having to work with the man, so I let it be."

"But all the other cameras, they worked fine didn't they? You must have tons of footage."

Stan's eyes cut over to Bobby and then back to me. "So what are you saying?" He rolled his eyes toward a shelf on a bookcase where a stack of DVDs was sitting.

"Oh, you men!" Bobby stood up and stamped her foot. "You may think you're being circumspect, but what he wants to know," she pointed at me, index finger straight and true, "is whether you," it was a glare that Stan got, "were smart enough to save all the output of all the recording devices that could possibly have recorded anything to do with Sean's death." She stopped for a second and you could see the coin drop. "Or Ford's retirement party." She rolled her eyes. "That he wouldn't come to. But now it appears he watched part of it and now would like a video of it, if you would be so kind.

"I'm leaving," she headed out the door. "Stan, send me the link to my video when it's ready."

I watched her as she walked down the hall. Right smart woman, I thought to myself.

"Oh and, Ford?" her voice dropped. "The discs you want are on the second shelf from the top."

Damned smart. I glanced over at Stan. He nodded toward her back, "That's one smart woman."

"Ya think?" I looked at the stack of DVDs sitting on the second shelf from the top of Stan's bookcase then looked at him. I think if we'd both been women Bobby's comment would have ended it. I would have picked up the discs and walked out. But I could be wrong. Anyway, we weren't, so we got there in our own way. A round-about way, I grant you.

I started off. "I don't know if I could come up with a reason I should have access to all the footage shot that day but I'd like to take a look at it."

Some phrases hang on in the language long after the literal meaning is gone. Footage? Like I could hold it up to the light and see images? Like you "dial" a phone?

Stan raised one eyebrow quizzically. "Are we talking about your retirement party? Didn't you ask me for a copy before you left? All the footage? For me not to bother and edit it? Now where did I put that note?" He began to shuffle through a stack of yellow Post-its.

"Did I?" I tried to keep from sounding surprised.

"You weren't sure what you were going to do with it. You were having second thoughts, I think. About the party." He nodded his head as if the words sounded convincing enough to persuade him. "Yeah, you were just taking out a little insurance. Just in case."

"Well, sure, now that you mention it. I was interested. Good of you to think of it."

"But you didn't email me about it because you didn't want to leave a record on the servers."

"Right!" I exclaimed.

"So I'm just going to have to go by the date on the note I took." Stan began writing on his yellow Post-it pad. "If anybody asks, that is. And who's going to?"

"I'm thinking you could get into a world of hurt giving me those disks," I whispered. I barely moved my lips.

Just as softly Stan muttered, "The guy who went around hurting people is dead, you idiot."

"Just because he's gone doesn't mean all's right with the world." I reached out to pick up the stack of disks and then dropped my hand. "I don't want to be seen walking around with a stack of disks in my hand. Got lunch plans?"

"I plan on eating." Stan patted his gut and smiled. "Can't let this shrink away to nothing. Worked too hard getting it this size."

"Chinese? The usual place?"

"Sure, I haven't been to the Happy Buddha yet this week."

I pointed toward the ceiling. "I'm going upstairs to look around and talk to some people. Come lunchtime, why don't you meet me there and bring those disks. Or," I corrected myself, "my retirement souvenir. My treat."

"You paying? Gosh, now I'm really getting hungry. Wonder if I can get Peking duck for lunch?"

I smiled. "Go wild, Stan. Just remember I'm a retiree, fixed income and all that."

Lunch and DVD delivery settled, I headed for the stairwell. The elevators in any public building should always be avoided if at all possible. Just remind yourself that all construction had to go out for bid—and was then bought from the lowest bidder. Look around. You'd be surprised at how much stuff has been supplied by companies that have since gone bankrupt. I headed up the stairs, wondering for the first time if that meant I should worry about the stairs as well.

I popped out of the stairwell on the fourth floor and ran straight into Don Larson, Mr. Security, if you will, waiting at the elevator.

"Crawford," Don frowned. "I thought you retired."

"What?" I feigned astonishment, "You've forgotten my retirement party? I'm hurt, hurt I tell you! I'd have thought at least the dead body would have stuck in your mind for a while. What with you being the head of security and all."

Don looked like he'd just bitten a green persimmon. "Comedian. I wasn't his bodyguard. That's not the kind of security I do and you know it. What are you doing here?"

"Don," I reminded him, "it's a public building. That means the public has access to it. When I retired I didn't retire from being a member of the public. Now Sean? Yeah, I'd have to say that he has retired from being a member of the public."

Don and I had never gotten along. It wasn't that he served in the first Gulf War while I had draft-dodged out of going to Vietnam by joining the Reserve. I've got good friends who served. No, I just didn't like his attitude toward life and he didn't like mine.

"I wouldn't count you as one of his admirers." The elevator chimed and the door opened.

"No," I agreed, "and I wouldn't have said you were one either." I shrugged my shoulders. "On that we ought to be able to agree."

"James F. Crawford, what are you doing here?" Veronica stepped out of the elevator.

A striking woman was Veronica Anson. Sometimes she was called Voni, her childhood nickname, but more often it was Veronica or Dr. Anson. I always thought of her as taller than she really was, maybe it was the way she carried herself. Dark hair to her shoulders, pure green eyes, not the muddied color called hazel. I had heard that tinted contacts helped make the color so clear, but never having seen her without them I couldn't testify one way or the other. Nor could I testify whether anything else had been artificially augmented. The clothes she wore were expensive, that I could see, but not tight. No, and no hint of cleavage from Veronica. Like Stan had said, Ice Queen. For that matter I called her that myself. I can't remember who said it first.

"Veronica," I hesitated, thinking what to say. I hadn't expected to see her today so I hadn't given it any thought. I had detested her fiancé. And I had wondered what was wrong with her, because from my point of view something must be deep down seriously wrong, wrong and twisted, for her to want to marry Sean. Hell, for her to put up with him. Of course he never had her bring him tea or heat up his soup in my presence. No, he had almost always treated her with respect—almost. Other than that obvious flaw, she seemed like a pleasant enough person. A fleeting memory popped up and slipped away before it was really recalled. "I don't know what to say."

"Don't say anything!" she said sharply. "I've heard it all: 'May the Lord comfort you in your time of sorrow,' 'God works in mysterious ways,' 'Time and the Lord will ease your pain,' and my personal favorite, 'I'll be happy to come and pray with you, just say the word.'" Her expression didn't change but her voice dripped venom.

She turned and looked at Don. "Oh, excuse me." Her tone clearly indicated that she wasn't sorry. I wondered if Don had been one of the ones who offered to pray. "Did you want to speak to Crawford?" The ice was back in her voice and she spoke with dismissive disdain, her speaking-to-the-peasants tone that had made her so popular with the staff.

Don took the hint and bolted for the elevator. "Got a meeting," came the voice somewhat muffled as the door closed.

Veronica turned back to look at me. I raised one eyebrow and said, "James F. Crawford? How did you come up with that? When my mom used my middle initial it meant I was getting close to her last nerve." I noticed she was dressed in black. Good observation I said to myself. I wonder if I would have noticed if she hadn't been wearing black.

"Oh," she flashed a token smile. "You forget who inherited your office. You left some plaques that had your full name on them."

"That explains that. For a moment I thought you must have seen my personnel file." And I still thought it. I hadn't left anything behind.

Sean had done that kind of thing too. Showing he had information he really shouldn't have had. Preening himself on being in the know, even when he wasn't. "Sorry about Sean." It was time to change the subject and I wasn't about to mention "passing" or "loss." I'd heard too much of that myself.

She winced. "Don't. I know you two weren't friends. It was a shame really, you're so much alike."

I bit my tongue. Maybe in some way Sean and I were alike. Alike in the hatred we held for one another. But other than that, I couldn't see it.

"There is going to be a memorial service. We're in negotiations with the provost about it."

"Really?" I said politely. "The provost?" Why Provost George I wondered. Seems like the chaplain would make more sense.

"The deputy director and I want to have the memorial in the new virtual multimedia room. He'll be interred in a family plot in Pennsylvania—his ashes will be, that is. So we thought to have a memorial service here."

Ah, I thought to myself, that's why no chaplain—and cremation. It's a small step from ass to ash. I repressed the thought and smile. "The one with the virtual wall? Have they finished it?"

"Yes, and Sean was trying to set up a grand opening ceremony before, before . . ." There was a catch in her voice and she cleared her throat before she spoke. "It was very important to him."

I raised my hand, "I'll testify to that." From the moment he'd walked in the door he'd been talking about glass caves, glass walls, glass floors, glass ceilings. Virtualizing everything from an amoeba to a human heart. And him always standing in the middle of it. Because of the cost, he'd had to settle for just one wall of multiple screens and projectors. And even then I could understand why she and Albert wanted to clear using the room with the provost.

"And that's why I wanted to talk to you," she stepped closer. All of a sudden she seemed smaller and softer. "We know, I mean Sean and I knew, that you're the best multimedia person in the state, if not the Southeast."

. . .

As I walked down the hall I puzzled over what I had done. How had she gotten me to agree to work on Sean's memorial service?

Work on? Hell, to produce it. How quickly I had gone from shocked speechlessness to grudging acceptance to almost excited anticipation. The lure of doing something that I do well? Maybe. The chance to play with half a million dollars worth of state-of-the-art equipment? Ouch, yeah that was part of it, if I was being honest. And why not be honest with myself? Certainly I needed to know the truth. Pride. It had done me in before and had gotten me again. I shook my head ruefully. I was proud of my work. Proud enough to think I would do a better memorial service than others even though I loathed the man.

I shook my head again. "Idiot," I said to the empty hall. And now I was going to have to meet with Albert Worthy, deputy director of the Department of Technology to get some footage on Sean. He was another one of the friends Sean had brought to campus. One of those who followed him from campus to campus as he climbed his own ladder of success.

I set out to find Peggy, the person I'd been looking for in the first place.

. . .

Instead of using the formal entrance to the executives' office suite, I headed for Sean's office via the back entrance. Peggy's "area" as they called it was right outside Sean's. The furniture had presented a little bit of a challenge when we were setting up the cameras, but we'd found a solution. You couldn't call it a receptionist's desk as she wasn't a receptionist. She was an administrative specialist by title, a title that didn't really tell you anything and had made it easier for Sean to bully her. He'd made a mockery of job titles since he arrived. In all honesty the university had always used job titles and job descriptions to confuse more than enlighten. To quote Human Resources, "The title doesn't have to be job specific. It should simply represent the family of responsibilities inherent in expected performance." HR once confessed they had consolidated a number of job titles just because it made it easier for them to respond to surveys. How their ability to respond to surveys furthered the goals of the university I never understood.

People who have worked at different places in various organizations over the years tell me that Human Resources, or Personnel, or whatever its current name is in new-speak is the most hated department in any organization. The only possible contender is Purchasing, which may be just as hated, but at least the department doesn't change its name with every new management trend. The only way employees in either one can demonstrate their authority is to say no. And so they do. I can't vouch for anywhere but the university, but it's certainly true here. Sean and HR had formed an unholy alliance that left employees feeling helpless and trapped because, in many ways, they were.

. . .

Peggy saw me over the ledge that bordered her desk. She was small and dark, full of nervous energy. She was cute. My guess was that she'd been cute all her life and gave every indication that she was going to continue to be cute. She hopped up and scooted around the desk.

"Crawford, can you believe it? Why I told Harold, but you know Harold." I always felt like I'd joined a conversation that was already in progress when I talked to Peggy. I don't know Harold but had given up trying to correct her. She rattled on,

"He just pats my head and says that things could be worse. As if they weren't already." She reached forward and hugged me.

I'm not a hugger or a person who initiates hugs. Not at work anyway. I figure it's not a real professional way to handle yourself, not to mention that you just might find out you've hugged the wrong person. But Peggy was a hugger and I knew better than to fight it. "He was an awful man. Disgusting. The way he was always touching the female employees as if he didn't know better.

"In fact," she dropped her voice, "I probably shouldn't tell you this because it is really naughty. You know those awful turtleneck sweaters he used to wear? I didn't think of it myself, but I promised not to quote her. Anyway, I said I thought he looked hideous in them, and she said, and I quote, 'It looks like someone had pulled the foreskin down and revealed him for the prick he is!'" She giggled and covered her mouth. "Get it?"

I admitted I "got it" and immediately began to wonder who had been clever and "naughty" enough to come up with the comment. I mean he was a prick, and to those with a certain imagination, a turtleneck—Sean's bald head—yeah, I could see it.

"So we all know what he was like and now he's dead and everybody is saying that it was the potato salad. Oh, Crawford, I'm so glad you're here I don't know who else to tell. Harold says it's nothing to worry about and I should just forget about it. I'd tell somebody here if there was anybody I could trust—but I can trust you, can't I?"

If Sean had been run over by a bus while walking across the street would that have made it easier to understand I wondered. Or maybe if a tree fell on him or lightning hit him? I patted her shoulder. "Trust me, Peggy, dead is dead, no matter how it happened. We can't all die of old age. Food poisoning is just another way to die."

"I do trust you. I always have. I don't know why, but I do. But you don't know, nobody knows, what I know." She broke the hug to tap her chest with her open palm. "I know it wasn't the potato salad."

"Now, Peggy," I glanced around the room knowing about the hidden microphones and cameras. "You need to be careful what you say and who might overhear you."

She waved her hands dismissively. "Oh, Crawford, I haven't told you the worst part of it." She tossed her hair. "Everybody is assuming that he ate the potato salad just because that's what made the others sick. Isn't that silly of them? It wasn't the potato salad. It couldn't have been. I know. I know because I made up a plate for him and he never ate it! I found it untouched in his office after they took him off in an ambulance."

"You fixed him a plate of food?" Having said that, I stood there with my jaw hanging open—slack-jawed and drooling. "I thought you hated bringing him tea?"

She drew herself up straight to her towering height of say—maybe five feet, with heels. "Well, of course I hated bringing him his tea but this was different. He never ate while a party was going on—afraid to get caught with his mouth full—and if he waited until the end of the party all the really good treats would be gone.

"But Crawford," she looked up at me with a puzzled expression on her face, "if he didn't eat any of the food what killed him?"

I was still trying to fathom the difference between making a plate of food for somebody and making a cup of tea. All I could do was shake my head and mumble something about how he must have snacked while talking to people or somebody gave him a bite. There was no telling. Baffled by her logic I beat a hasty retreat.

CHAPTER 5
THURSDAY LUNCH

I met Stan at the Happy Buddha a little before noon. He was already there but had waited for me in the parking lot. Without a word he handed me the stack of DVDs, I took them, walked back to my car, and put them safely inside. Stan had started walking toward the restaurant as I had headed back to my car. I stopped and looked around before following him across the lot to the Happy Buddha.

The restaurant is in a strip mall just off the main street that cuts through campus east and west. The university had led the effort to clean up the areas just off campus. No, let me be precise, the university wanted to spruce up the appearance of the major access roads people (read alumni and donors, correction, donors current and prospective) took when they came to the campus. As far as I could tell they didn't give a tinker's damn about how the neighborhoods off the main streets looked. But the burger joints, sports bars, party stores, gay bars, head shops, live music bars, fast food places, frat bars, souvenir stores, sorority bars, bookstores, all the places that had been there for ages and looked it weren't part of the greater plan. Despite the fact the natives called it "the Strip," there were no strip joints. If they looked like places Barbie and Ken, or rather Barbie's and Ken's parents, would approve of they had a chance of survival; places that Bubba, Ozzy, Daisy, Stoner, Goth girl, and Jamal would find comfortable, not so much.

They wanted the area to appeal to parents who were sending their children and their money somewhere, somewhere safe and sanitary. They were lucky students still wanted to enroll, as far as I was concerned. But you've got to remember my roots. My generation, my colleagues had coined the phrase "don't trust an-ybody over thirty." I was still comfortable with that, only I dropped the "over thirty" part.

The university had trotted out their long-range plan before the board of trustees (after numerous behind-the-scenes conver-sations) and had gotten approval to develop a plan. They had several informal "information gathering" meetings with the city's zoning and licensing board, councilmen, councilwomen, and real estate developers.

And then, surprise, surprise, the university discovered that they actually owned most of the property under consideration. They had been buying properties through proxies for decades and turned out to be the landlord for most of the places that they now wanted to disappear. As one disgruntled bar owner who discovered that his lease wasn't going to be renewed put it, "Hell, they've been holding their noses and taking my money for two decades! How come their sense of smell got so good now?"

So the university "exercised their rights as property owners" and booted the small businesses out and leased the land to de-velopers who promised to create "upscale shopping experienc-es." The Happy Buddha sat in one of the first of those designed-to-be-enticing shopping areas, where the turnover was rapid as business after business tried to make a go of it only to fail, una-ble to pay the rents that were needed to cover the cost of the trendy, upscale look. Most of the shops were large chains, with the occasional exception, like the Happy Buddha.

In a college town there is one guaranteed way to run a suc-cessful restaurant. Provide pretty good food, large servings, and low prices. The lower the better. Don't worry about the ambi-ence—clean is nice, but you don't have to go overboard. And don't make it too comfortable, you need to turn the tables. Just make it quick, tasty, and plentiful.

I stepped inside and took off my sunglasses. I noted, not for the first time, that, unlike in most restaurants and shops in Alabama, I was not met with the bracing cold of a meat locker. The owners knew that people would come for the quality and quantity of the reasonably priced food. But they didn't want their clients to use the restaurant as respite from the Alabama heat. Lingering was not encouraged, and they managed to turn over the tables in a brisk manner.

Stan was sitting in a booth staring at an open menu. I slid in across from him. "Something new on the menu? Something that wasn't there last week?" I picked the other menu up off the table and opened it. I ran my finger down the lunch menu. "Nope, General chicken is still General chicken."

Stan slapped the menu down on the table and said, "I don't like it. Makes me uncomfortable."

"General chicken?" I was shocked. You eat lunch with a guy for ten years, usually going to the same places week after week, and you get a feel for what he's going to order. "I've never known you to order it. You never order it. So how could it make you uncomfortable?"

Stan looked at me like I'd grown two heads. Two additional heads. "I'm not talking about the food."

"Ready?" The waiter had appeared at our booth.

"Yeah," said Stan distractedly. "Chicken and mushrooms, steamed rice, hot and sour soup, and water, no lemon."

The waiter who must have used shorthand to write down the order turned to face me. Interesting, three earrings in one ear, none in the other, and I'm not sure what the tattoo crawling up his neck was supposed to represent. Fortunately, his T-shirt hid most of it. Even better, as far as I was concerned, he hadn't said, "Hi, I'm Brian and I'm going to be your server today!" He really hadn't said anything other than "Ready?"

"Uh, sweet tea, General chicken, fried rice, hot and sour soup." I'd given up trying not to get the egg roll. I can't remember if the menu says "no substitutions" but it didn't matter. The waiters were almost robotic in their uniform desire to hand out an egg roll.

"The memorial service Veronica wants." He pointed at a bowl on the table. "Do you know what they call these crunchy things?" He took a few and popped them in his mouth as I shook my head no. "Me neither, but they sure are great in soup."

"What about the service makes you uncomfortable?" I followed his lead and took a handful of whatever the crunchy things were called. "Or is it just the fact that there's going to be one? Oh, right." Stan had always been more uncomfortable around tragedy than I was. I put it down to the age difference. When I was his age I was probably just as uncomfortable. Nothing a few deaths in the family wouldn't cure. "It's the service being on campus."

"And in the new room!" Yep, it was bothering him.

"I wondered about that too, but she's got her reasons. Veronica, that is." As we continued to nibble, I confessed. "I just talked to her today and said, God knows why, that I'd help with the video part. You know that's why she wants to have it in the new room with the virtual wall?"

Stan's eyes widened. "You said you would help?"

"Yeah, one minute I'm wondering what to say to her that wouldn't be a lie and the next thing I know I'm agreeing to put together the memorial video. Don't know how it happened but it did. I agreed to produce a video for the memorial service. The provost agreed to speak a few words and the service is being held in the new multimedia room in the computer center." I shrugged my shoulders. "I don't know how she does it.

"Still haven't decided when to have it other than some day next week. This weekend is out. Victoria Moore, the provost's assistant, will be working with Peggy to coordinate it. Oh," that reminded me, "I'm going to need any footage of Sean that you've got for the video."

The waiter returned with our drinks and two egg rolls on a stack of saucers. We watched as he set the drinks in front of us. And sat wordless while he rolled one egg roll off the saucer onto another one and set them before us. Sometimes the brown, crisp cylinders rolled too well and went off the saucer onto the table, adding excitement to an otherwise dull meal, but not this time.

I looked up at the waiter, "Spicy mustard?" He nodded.

Stan reached for the red sauce and spooned some onto his saucer. "Videos of Sean? Got tons of the stuff. Come by tomorrow and I'll loan you a hard drive full of it." He dipped one end of the egg roll into the sauce and, with it halfway to his mouth, stopped and stared at me. He lowered the roll. "OK, I get it. I see what you're doing. Very Machiavellian of you. Clever." He took a bite out of the egg roll, took a couple of chews and said, "If I can help, let me know. I mean if I can help you help her, that is."

I raised one eyebrow, the left one if it matters. "What are you talking about?"

"Befriending your enemies like that. Must be suggested in *The Prince* right? Giving them a false sense of security."

The waiter reappeared with the spicy mustard. As he set the squeeze bottle on the table he said, "I think it's from *The Art of War.*" He hadn't had to go very far at all, not even out of earshot.

I looked up at the waiter and reminded myself for the ten-thousandth time that you can't always tell about people from appearances. Got to judge them by what they do, not what they look like they could do. "I plead ignorance. Like I said, I don't know why I agreed to help her. But the worst thing I know about her is her taste in boyfriends."

"Her?" the waiter said. He sounded a little bit disappointed.

"Right." I squeezed a little dollop of the mustard onto the saucer and carefully dipped one edge of the egg roll into it.

"You offered to help a female? Hardwired in your genes." He turned and walked down the aisle between the tables. I decided that he must be a psych major—probably a grad student going for his PhD.

Relieved to no longer be the subject of psychiatric analysis, I bit into the egg roll, swallowed, and felt the back of my sinuses explode and then flames shoot out of my nose. I blinked my eyes. Hard. Why, I wondered, do I do that to myself?

Stan watched my eyes water and pushed the mustard bottle away from him. "It's a fresh batch then."

Over the years we'd come up with various theories about why the degree of spiciness of the mustard varied so widely. Some days it was so mild that Stan would mix it with the sweet and sour sauce to use and I'd slather it all over the egg roll. Other times it was like today's batch. One bite and that was it. We hadn't been able to decide whether it lost its zest as it aged or got more concentrated. We could have asked, I suppose, but we were guys and the thought hadn't occurred to us. Just like the crispy things. I could argue that the waiters and waitresses wouldn't have known the answer, but the fact is we didn't ask.

"Right. Cleared those sinuses out."

"So, why use the new room?"

I had wondered if Stan was going to come back to that. "Because it's an example of what he was striving to do here. Part of the legacy that he's left behind," I quoted.

"What? Kicking people out of their offices and into the basement to make room for something that didn't need to be built? At least not in our building it didn't. Who wants to make cutting-edge presentations or perform in-depth analysis in the computer center? Why not the new engineering complex? Or the biology building where they're actually using virtualization?"

The soup got delivered next. No excitement here. The waitstaff hadn't figured out a way to deliver the soup that added an extra touch of peril. There was just the possibility of hot liquid getting dumped in your lap.

"Same old argument and I'm still a member of the choir." I picked up a handful of those crunchy things and dropped them in the soup. "It shouldn't have been built in Alexander Hall, but it was."

"Yeah," said Stan, "because in his building he didn't have to deal with the department heads who would have demanded some say in what he was doing." He started in on his soup as well. "Maybe then the raised floor would have enough room for electrical cables."

The first time I had hot and sour soup had been at the end of a long and tiring day. My wife and I had moved from an apartment to our first house and had been young enough and foolish enough and poor enough to undertake such a project without professional help. I've loved it ever since. It doesn't have to be great like that first bowl was. Good is good enough.

"Oh, there's enough room for a few cables. It's the plugs on either end that don't fit." Sean had talked about how the room, his room, would set the standard for all the rooms to follow.

Those of us on the design committee whose valid concerns had been scorned, ridiculed, and dismissed had come to agree. Indeed, the room would stand as a model of what not to do. The fact that if we'd purchased the flooring system that was cheaper, but not Sean's choice, we'd have had more room and an easier configuration to work with was yet another example of his tremendous leadership skills.

I mentioned that Veronica had said how Sean had considered me the best video guy in the Southeast. Stan replied that Voni would rather lie than tell the truth. Unfortunately I had to agree with him.

We drifted off the subject of how poorly designed and overpriced the new room was and made idle shoptalk over the rest of the soup and the entrees. Along the way Stan came up with some ideas about how to use some of the new features that were built into the room and I left with a number of interesting approaches to take.

. . .

As I pulled up to my house I saw Mary's car and realized that I'd forgotten that it was her day to clean the house. She worked at the university; in fact that's how I met her. Cleaning Services is the term they use nowadays, but most of us still call it housekeeping. I think the workers were better off as housekeepers. Some MBA type decided that the university didn't need to provide those services themselves. No, the university had to realize that it couldn't provide every service. So they fired all the housekeepers and hired a company to supply "cleaning services," and that company tried to hire all the old housekeepers that had been fired. Of course they couldn't pay them what they'd been earning or provide similar benefits. That had gone over well.

What the MBA type hadn't realized was that the university already wasn't paying those people enough to live on. Shoot they had split the work up into two shifts, one in the early morning, the other at the end of the school day. They wouldn't let anybody work both shifts, so nobody worked enough hours to qualify for benefits . . . or retirement. So how did they make a living? Working privately for staff, faculty, and townies of course. I'm not saying that the university had deliberately created this pool of underemployed domestic workers just so the underpaid faculty and staff could employ them. No, I think it was an unexpected benefit that nobody even realized was there until it was threatened with extinction.

That, of course, is what the MBA hadn't considered. Can you imagine how many vice presidents, deans, directors, department heads, and associate professors had their homes cleaned, clothes washed and ironed, food cooked, and children cared for by those university employees who had just been fired by Mr. MBA? I've never seen the university reverse itself so quickly.

I was smiling at the memory as I got out of my car and started toward the door. I'd known Mary Keith for years before my wife and I had started earning enough to be able to afford a part-time housekeeper of our own. Mary had the early shift and I always liked to get to work early so we'd had years of idle talk about the weather and would Friday ever get here and so on. She'd had a full slate of private clients but she had agreed to work us in when I finally asked. Come to think on it, she must be semiretired by now. I wondered for a moment who the others were she still worked for.

"Mary," I bellowed as I entered the door. "Mary! I'm sorry, I forgot what day it was!"

"And am I supposed to be surprised?" Her quiet voice was a counterpoint to my shout. I had come into the house via the laundry room and she was standing in the doorway from the den into the kitchen, hands on her hips. Lord, I knew that look. I was in for it now. I began to wonder what else I had done—or left undone.

"You getting old and forgetful!" She glared at me for a moment. "I told you when Miz Eleanor died, God rest her soul, that I'd stay on and help out. But this is getting old, Mr. Crawford. Mighty old!"

"Now, Mary," I held up my hands in surrender. "Something came up and . . ."

"Don't you 'now, Mary' me!" She snapped back. "Something came up! Well I guess it did. A man you dislike so much that you'd quit a good job just to get away from dies at your retirement party from eating po-ta-to salad!" She crossed her arms. "And then your policeman friend Captain Ward comes visiting you, first thing in the morning. All that going on and you ain't got the common decency to be here to tell me about it?"

I don't know what it's like to have been born, bred, and grown up in a small town. I grew up in one of Alabama's larger cities. So if everybody knows everybody else's business in a municipality this size, what more do they know in a small town? Oh, I don't suppose everybody in Shelbyville knew that a policeman had been at my house this morning. But I'd bet you that everybody who was interested knew, or soon would know. I wondered if I needed to tell Jim that his unmarked car had been spotted. Considering he knew better than I what a small town Shelbyville was I guessed not.

"It was food poisoning," I started.

"Well, ain't that a surprise! What else is the whole town talking about? Least it's a change from talking football."

When Mary got riled it was better to go ahead and let her speak. I had learned that lesson over the years. Trying to interrupt was the worst thing you could do.

"If a man just drops dead at work of a heart attack it's a three-day-wonder. But a man dying from eating food prepared by Food Services? The university's Food Services? Some hotshot from out of town who's been throwing his weight around? And drop dead from potato salad? This town will be talking about it for months, if not years." She shook her head ruefully. "There's no use saying 'God rest his soul' 'cause that man didn't deserve a good night's sleep much less a restful soul. I don't mean to tell the Lord what to do, but that man . . . you think he treated you 'professionals' bad? Lord, the tales I've heard."

She seemed as if she was through venting so I ventured a comment. "Yep, I've heard the man needed killing."

"Don't you go around saying things like that Mr. Crawford. It's the Lord's decision, not man's."

"It's just an observation, Mary. There are lots of bad people out there, some of them so bad that most people think the world would be better off without them. Just 'cause they 'need killing' doesn't mean somebody is going to kill them.

"The man died of food poisoning—an allergic reaction to something he ate. I don't think Jim Ward even knew what he was supposed to be allergic to."

Mary cocked her head and looked at me to see if I was kidding. "That woman of his told the doctors at the hospital that he was allergic to potato salad—or something in potato salad, anyway. Least that's what the orderly in the room heard her say and he's a truthful boy. Question is, why'd he eat it? Food Services' potato salad?" She snorted. "Freshman boys got more sense than to eat that stuff." She paused, "Well, freshman girls for sure."

Mary stepped into the laundry room and picked up her hand-bag. "There's a basket of clean clothes on the dryer that I'm not folding since you don't care. The ironing is hung up. Put it where you want it. Tan is outside wishing somebody would come out and play with her and The Black is asleep on top of the freezer. I've got to go."

With that she swept by me and was out the door, sailing down the driveway. "What about your check?" I shouted after her.

She waved her hand over her head not bothering to turn around. "I took what you owe me out of the cookie jar."

I was sitting with my elbows on the kitchen counter staring into my third cup of coffee muttering to myself when The Black appeared on the counter, walked over, and head-butted my arm. "You're not supposed to be on the counter," I told him, realizing at that moment that I'd been talking to myself out loud. The cat cocked his head slightly and sat down facing me. His green eyes didn't blink. "Really, you know you're not supposed to be on the counter." Eleanor and I had always tried to keep the dogs off the furniture. Never had cats to deal with. Neither of us had ever thought of ourselves as "cat people." I reached over and poked The Black in the chest with my finger and he in turn gently bit it. "Come on, play fair," I said. "Get off the counter. Give me a break. I had a rough night."

I got up to push him off and saw that the phone was blinking. I had voicemail. I pushed the cat toward the edge of the counter. "Who called? Must have been while I was in the shower." TB ignored my question and leapt to the floor.

There were two messages. One was from Albert Worthy at the university. Dr. Anson had told him that I was going to put together the memorial tribute to Sean. He said he had a bunch of footage of Sean at events over the years that might be helpful and asked me to come by and pick them up. His usual heartiness was muted, in fact he sounded a little depressed. But I guess he had good reason to be depressed since his friend and mentor had just died. Sean was the reason Albert was here at the university. I stopped for a second. I was retired; should I say "here at the university" since I wasn't there any more? I pondered on that for half a heartbeat and decided I'd have to ask.

The second message was from Jim Ward, calling to check up on me, in his own way. I had left a message on his phone saying that his car had been busted—even casual observers knew it was owned by a cop. His message was something to the effect that he hoped having a policeman's car parked in front of my house hadn't damaged my reputation with the neighbors. On that cheery note, I decided to make two phone calls on my own. I got Stan and reminded him of the footage he'd promised. He said he'd leave it at the desk since he was going to be in and out today.

The other call put an end to my plans for lunch as my friend informed me that today was a particularly bad day on campus for going out to lunch. It was a night game and since neither of us were going, we'd agreed on supper tomorrow with drinks and appetizers beforehand. Come over while the game was being played, which was much easier, and safer, than afterward. Too much school spirit got imbibed by too many people who were either too young to know better or too old to be pretending they were that young again. And I got to ask my question about whether a retiree was entitled to say things like "here at the university." I'd get the answer on Saturday.

. . .

The drive to the university was almost automatic after all these years. Once you got to campus things were a bit different. Dealing with traffic had always been a challenge at the university. I timed my arrival for the middle of a class period. That way I missed the students who were going to arrive just before class started and the ones who were going to leave as soon as class ended. The rest of the students weren't on the roads. The streets were almost empty except for a few faculty and staff members slipping out for an early lunch. That was the other part of the timing. You give up a parking spot only when you've got a good chance of getting another. Employees who come back from lunch early have a much better chance of finding a parking spot than those who don't.

We used to laugh about how the parking passes were like hunting permits. Just because you bought a permit didn't mean you were going to find a parking space. Then the cost of the permits kept going up until it wasn't funny anymore. I pulled into the lot and grabbed the first available parking space. Albert's office was on the top floor, but I took the stairs anyway. I had been stuck in the elevator once and didn't care to do it again. Besides, the exercise would do me good.

I stopped at the landing and waited to catch my breath. I had overlooked the fact that I no longer climbed those stairs four or more times a day, five days a week. I realized that the land is pretty flat where I've been walking. I need to go a different direction and run into some hills.

. . .

I paused for a second outside of Albert's office. When you work at a place for as long as I did, you get to see a lot of people coming and going, moving in and out of offices, buildings, jobs. Albert was now inhabiting the office of the legendary Lennie. A man so confident in himself that he refused to apply for a job that he thought should be his. As it turned out, the director thought so too. I wondered if the office was as disappointed in its current occupant as I was. Particularly in light of who used to be there.

I tapped on the doorjamb and Albert looked up. The impression I had gotten over the phone was right. He looked tired and a little worried. As far as I could tell, Albert was a far better manager than Sean but, just like with Veronica, I had to question his judgment in electing to work with him. I realize I am biased.

"Crawford, thanks for coming."

He stood up, came out from behind his desk, and put out his hand. I took it. It bothers me to shake hands with people I really don't care for. I know the origins of the handshake. How we started shaking hands to show that we weren't holding weapons and to check and see if the other guy was. The fact of the matter is that nowadays to refuse to shake hands with a man is a very serious insult. And I wasn't ready to be that insulting to Albert. Not yet.

Albert was one of the hearty handshake guys—compensating for his slight build I imagine. I rescued my hand before he did too much damage.

"I should be thanking you. It's going to make my life lots easier having way more material than I need to work with."

"Right! I can see that." Albert bobbed his head in agreement and I wondered, not for the first time, why he dyed his hair. But then I wondered why anybody did. "I've just about got everything together." He pointed to one of those boxes movers use to store the contents of filing cabinets. "There's a brief description of what's on the disk, the purpose of the event, who's there that's important, a copy of Sean's speech or remarks, background on the award, a list of who attended, index to the pictures, pretty much everything that's important."

I raised both eyebrows and glanced at the box and then back at Albert. "Wow," was all I could say. I had seen press agents who were nowhere near as organized. Hell, I had known people whose dissertation research wasn't as organized as this. I was so stunned that I nearly asked where the list of the contents was, just to make a joke.

"The only thing I haven't got for you is the complete listing of the events covered by the contents sorted chronologically and then ranked by relative importance." He looked at my stunned countenance. "That would help you, wouldn't it?"

"Oh, yes, it certainly would." I said somewhat weakly. What had I been expecting? A box of clippings to sort through? Yes, that's exactly what I'd expected and a lot closer to what I usually got.

"I'm printing it out now. I don't have a color printer here, so I've sent it to the printer on the second floor. It's near the new multimedia room. I understand that you're planning on using it for the memorial service?" His voice made it a question.

"That's what Veronica said she wanted." I shrugged my shoulders. "I'm just doing what I'm told."

"I'm aware of Dr. Anson's preferences but I understand that it's up to Provost George whether the room can be used."

I heard the rebuke in his voice for my familiarity in referring to Dr. Anson as "Veronica."

"Well it was Rufus's money that paid for it." I had just called the provost by his first name. I wondered if he was going to re-buke me again. "I think that's between the two of them." I glanced down at my wrist as if the time was important to me. I was glad to see I'd remembered to put a watch on it. "You men-tioned a document?"

Our eyes met for a second then he turned away. "It should have printed by now. Wait here, I'll go get it. I should make sure you understand the keys."

I watched him lock a file cabinet before he walked out of his office. He paused at the door as if he was tempted to lock it too, but thought better of it. I didn't take offense. Everybody knew that Albert believed locks were put there to be used. It might have been the first time he'd left this office without locking it behind him.

I then glanced around the room. It had never been my office but like I said I knew some of the prior occupants. I wondered for a moment what had happened to Lennie's nutcracker collection. I glanced around looking at how Albert had decorated the office. Everything was new. Even the antique football programs were new, in the sense that he had bought them after coming to the university. All the knickknacks and stuff were new and university related. "Themed" an interior designer would say.

The room was decorated to look like the resident was a life-long, diehard university supporter. Who's got more money than sense I thought; that Steuben baseball with the logo on it must have cost a bundle. I'd heard about them, but never seen one. Heck, we weren't even that good in baseball. His key chain was on the edge of his desk and it too was distinctive with a university fob and color-coded keys.

I glanced out the window that overlooked the parking lot and saw several empty spots. Must be close to noon. They'd start filling back up soon enough—well, not all of them. I'd forgotten that today was Friday. There'd be people taking a half-day off to make it a long weekend. There was a home football game tomorrow—the recreational vehicles would be pulling onto campus this afternoon and parking lots all over campus would transform into campgrounds. Campers, grills, coolers, even TV satellite dishes would pop us as the pregame partying started. It was a sight to behold.

I turned around and walked to the office doorway that opened onto Sean's "campus," the scene of my retirement party. I remembered having a camera mounted to capture this viewpoint. I glanced around the room checking to see if I could remember where we had hidden all the cameras and microphones.

"Here you go, Crawford." Albert bustled up flipping through five or six sheets of paper covered in different colors. "I think we'd better go over this. It's more complicated than I remembered." He didn't even glance over to the spot where Sean had collapsed. Maybe he couldn't. I took my copy of the pages and tried to make sense out of the information there. Too bad there weren't any color keys for life. What's important and what's not.

. . .

It took a little while, but I caught on to Albert's labeling system. I had to admit he'd done a hell of a job and told him so. I had enough background to fill hours, and I was planning on keeping it quite a bit shorter than that. I'd have to check with Rufus, pardon me, the provost, to see how long he wanted this memorial service to be. After all, as full of himself as Sean was, his tenure here hadn't lasted very long, nor had he accomplished that much, despite what he claimed. Except, I corrected myself, for making people hate him. I'm not sure if anybody had ever before done that so successfully so quickly.

I picked up the box, thereby avoiding another handshake, and said. "Thanks for your help, Albert."

"You're welcome." He replied absentmindedly as if he was thinking about something else. "Do you remember Dr. Anson saying," he caught himself, "oh, that's right, you weren't at the party—never mind."

I thanked him again for his help, and headed toward the help desk where Stan had left the portable hard drive. It being lunchtime there were only student workers behind the desk so I was able to get the disk with a minimum of chit-chat. There was just enough room in the box to hold the drive and external power source. I was glad Stan had thought to provide that too. Nothing more useless than a hard drive without power—for accessing data anyway.

I left the service desk and headed to the stairwell next to the elevator. If you're wondering why the help desk in the computer center wasn't located on the first floor and at an entrance students used all I can say is that it *had* been.

When I got to the door I recognized the woman dressed in a university-mandated maintenance uniform standing at the elevator door. "Delia! How you doing?" I said and added a big grin. She'd lived through some tough times and didn't have much patience for those who didn't enjoy life.

She jumped and laughed. "Bless me. Don't you be sneaking up on people like that!"

"I wasn't sneaking," I protested. "You must have been day-dreaming."

"Huh," she said, "and how likely is that?" Still, she must have had her mind on something because it took her another second for things to register. "Mr. Crawford, what are you doing here? Wasn't your retirement party just the other day? I had to clean up after it, anyways, everything Food Services didn't."

The elevator chimed and the door opened. The elevator was empty. "Come on," said Delia, "I'll give you a ride." She stepped in and held the door.

"I don't know about this. How good is your driving?" So Delia hadn't come to the party, but she had been there later.

"I still ain't never figured out how to make it go sideways. Up and down I can handle. How about you?" She looked at me and jerked her head backward. "Get in the car."

The box was getting heavier the longer I held it. I gave up on the stairwell and followed Delia into the car.

Delia Lewis was a hard-working, God-fearing, seen-it-all kind of woman. We weren't friends, quite. But over the years we'd done each other favors. She hadn't wanted to be the one to turn in her supervisor, who was stealing, because he would have blamed it on her. With the help of a well-placed camera, he lost his job. I had had problems of my own that she'd helped with. We both took pride in doing a good job and didn't much care for those who didn't.

"You should be glad you didn't come to my retirement party. You've heard what happened?"

Delia cocked her head and looked at me. The elevator door closed. "Retirement made you stupid?" she said.

I forgot to mention that she didn't suffer fools gladly. Rather than argue about if I was any more stupid than I had been before retirement I decided that silence was the best response.

"What are you doing back here? Hadn't you figured out that you are the red-headed stepchild?" She looked up nervously at the ceiling of the elevator, clearly wondering what was above the oh-so-innocent lattice-work.

"Delia, the elevator isn't—" I stopped before saying it wasn't bugged. Just because I hadn't figured out a way to do it didn't mean that others hadn't. In fact, I wondered if I had ignored a perfectly reliable power source by not tapping into the lights. "Came by to pick up some stuff I need."

She glared at me. "Don't tell me what the man can do and what he can't do. Besides I don't trust elevators."

I nodded at her. "I stand corrected." We rode the rest of the way down in silence.

She started talking as we got outside. Not looking at me but talking to me. We were standing on a small covered patio that served as the entrance to the building. I put the box down. "That box you're carrying tells me that what I hear is true. You been talking to somebody you'd best be staying away from."

"I have?" Somehow I couldn't see Albert inspiring that kind of warning.

"You not the only one made happy by that man's death. That she-wolf is too, even if she tries not to show it."

"She-wolf?" It took a second but then I got it, female wolves go by the same name female dogs do. Delia didn't like to cuss. She was talking about Veronica and making her feelings clear. "But they were going to get married," I exclaimed.

"Married!" Her voice was sharp. "And whose idea was that? Not hers I'm telling you. I've seen her look at him while nobody's watching. Nobody but me that is. And she thinks I'm a nobody." She looked squarely at me. "Mr. Crawford, I've seen hate. And I saw it there in her eyes. Fear and hate."

"Really?" I am constantly being surprised by how multifaceted people are. "I've always thought of her as the Ice Queen, you know, cold and cruel and not scared of anything. And that's what they saw in each other—the cruelty."

"Men. What you using to think with? She pretty enough I grant you but she doesn't like men. Not that one, anyway. Oh, she came when he called, but she didn't like it. I saw her cringe when he touched her. Made her skin crawl, I'd say. Ice Queen or not, she didn't want that man. And she's glad now that she's out of it." Delia shook her head. "There ain't no tear-stained tissues in that woman's trash."

I stared at Delia eye to eye. We were about the same height. "That's not what everybody else is saying."

Her voice mocked me. *"That's not what everybody—* What I'm trying to tell you is that she's not your friend or mine either. For the rest," she shrugged, "all I know is what I seen. You saw ice, I saw hate. Don't matter what you think or me either. He's dead. She's rid of him." She pointed her finger at me. "And you should stay away from her too!"

"Delia, I'll do my best." She nodded and walked away.

I was staring after her wondering about her warning when Stan walked up with that satisfied look of having come back from lunch.

"You get the hard drive?" The toothpick in his mouth bobbed up and down.

"Yeah, thanks for your help. And thanks for the power source. Saved me from having to come back and borrow it too. Where was lunch today? That Mexican place?"

"Nope. Went home and foraged for food."

"Turkey burgers?" It was a guess. Sometimes he'd grill a couple of frozen turkey burgers for lunch. Evidently they came with some kind of thermometer or sensor that would pop up when the burger was done. I'd never tried them, being something of a purist when it comes to burgers, but Stan never gave up promoting them. They were low in something that translated into being healthy for you. I had my doubts but I kept them to myself.

"No!" Stan's voice held a note of outrage. "The big box store stopped carrying them and I haven't been able to find them anywhere else. Have you seen them?"

"Are they the ones wrapped in bacon?" Despite Stan's encouragement I had never even looked for them and wouldn't have recognized them if I had seen them.

"No, those are turkey filets."

I shrugged my shoulders. "Can't help you then. Thanks again for those DVDs yesterday. Haven't had a chance to look at them yet."

"Good thing that you got them yesterday morning. Kept me from having to lie."

"You got a problem with lying all of a sudden? Did you forget everything I taught you? What happened?"

"You always told me the best way to lie is to keep it simple. So when Albert came by my office yesterday to ask if there was any footage of your retirement party left on the cameras I told him that I'd wiped the hard drives and I didn't have copies. I sure as hell didn't tell him you had copies of the whole party."

"Wonder why he wanted it?"

"Oh, he murmured something about getting it for Food Services. They're claiming that somebody must have tampered with the potato salad or whatever it was that made everybody sick. Albert was wondering if there was a chance we could have caught that," Stan winked. "I had to remind him that we hadn't started recording until right before Sean collapsed. So even if I hadn't erased it, we wouldn't have caught anybody tampering with the food." Stan shrugged. "Voni didn't bother to offer an explanation when she called this morning. She just wanted to know if any footage existed—yes or no."

"Sounds like the old Ice Queen. How did she take no for an answer?"

"Oh, I told her that Albert had already asked if there were any recordings and I had told him no. Once again," he wagged his finger at me admonishingly, "keeping the lie as simple as possible."

"Ah, very wise. Learned your lessons well, you have. Proud I am." I don't do a great Yoda imitation but I try. Come to think of it, maybe I should stop—or get better.

Stan smiled. "Need help with the box?"

"No, I can manage it."

"OK, I'd better get back to work. See you later."

I headed out into the parking lot and was halfway to my car when I heard a shout. "Mr. Crawford, Mr. Crawford." With the box I was holding, it was hard to look around and see where the voice was coming from, but I recognized it easily.

"Don't be fussing at me, Gwen! I parked as legal as you please." Gwen Campbell had a voice that carried and so did I and for some reason we derived a little pleasure from bellowing at each other across parking lots. Since she enforced parking regulations in the lots near the computer center, we'd had plenty of opportunities.

"Now don't you be lying to me! I knows you retired. What you doing with an active faculty/staff parking sticker?"

She was standing right in front of me now, hands on her ample hips and a serious frown on her face. As short as she was, the box I was holding had blocked my view.

"I'm going to have to escort you to your car and confiscate that sticker. Don't matter that you paid for it. You not eligible anymore."

The early autumn heat, the weight of the box, and carrying on a conversation at the top of my lungs was beginning to wear on me. "Lord, Gwen, that's the letter of the law, not the spirit of it. You're sounding like my wife, God rest her soul." Eleanor had liked to follow rules, sometimes to my irritation.

"How long ago you lose your wife, Mr. Crawford?" She didn't look surprised that I was a widow.

"I didn't 'lose her,' she didn't 'pass,' and, no, I don't think 'God called her home.' She died. In a car wreck."

Gwen's face had frozen at my first words.

"It was five years ago, which is long enough for me not to act like a jerk about it when somebody asks." I shook my head. "Sorry, Gwen."

She nodded her head. "It's OK, Mr. Crawford. Usually we just joke around when we talk. I mean, I know you well enough to know your name and recognize that you know mine—and what that means. Hell, I think you might even know my last name."

"Campbell," I replied automatically. "I asked. Gwen Campbell, transportation specialist, right?

"It's all right. Everybody grieves different." She cocked her head and looked up at me. "You know, James Crawford," the smile had returned to Gwen's face, "most people don't bother to find out what the 'meter maid's' name is. There just might be more to you than I had thought."

I was still too rattled about my outburst to do more than thank her for forgiving me and go on to the car.

I put the box in the backseat of the car then slid into the driver's seat. Thoughtfully I folded up the sunshield that I'd put up before getting out. It was hot to the touch, but the steering wheel wasn't. Don't know why everybody who lives in the South doesn't use these reflecting screens. Guess it's the same reason people don't use seat belts. I had buckled mine without even thinking. It's just a small thing but it can make a difference. I cranked the car and felt the air conditioning kick in. I felt bad about snapping at Gwen, but she seemed to have forgiven me. At least she hadn't taken my parking pass away.

Glancing at my watch I realized that I needed to wait five minutes to miss the tidal ebb and flow of the traffic between class times. I wondered if the wristwatch was going the way of buggy whips. I'd heard about it on NPR. Today's kids no longer used wristwatches. The time was there on their cell phones, which they used constantly anyway, so there was no need to wear a watch. "Should have sold my Timex stock," I muttered to myself. Not that I owned any. At which point I remembered I'd turned off my cell phone before I went in to see Albert. Yes, there was a message. Maybe if I stopped wearing a watch I'd check my phone more often?

. . .

The call had been from Victoria, Provost George's assistant. She was trying to pin down what day next week the service was going to be. Seems she needed to know that in order to do her job. Dr. Anson had told her that it depended on when the video I was preparing would be ready. I had a hunch that there had been a little friction between Victoria and the Ice Queen—not that Victoria would admit to it.

I thought for a moment. Let's see. Today is, Friday. Can't do it this weekend, not only because there's not enough time, but the game is at home. And next weekend they'll be playing in South Carolina so the town will be filled with social events that couldn't compete with the football game: weddings, fundraisers, folk art shows, and everything else that had to get shoehorned into those "away" weekends. Even then you hoped that the game wouldn't be televised while your event was going on. I'd been to wedding receptions where the father of the bride had set up a big screen television in a side room so people could slip in and check on the game. For that matter, I chuckled to myself, there were tales of ministers who performed ceremonies with a radio earplug discretely tucked in their ear. But I thought the stories of the minister yelling "Praise the Lord he scored!" as the bride and groom kissed was just a good story that had got better with the telling and retelling.

Wednesday. I'm not sure what mental processes went into that day popping into my head. Monday was too soon, Friday too late, and Tuesday and Thursday were the most popular days for students to take classes so I guess it made sense. I could work on the memorial stuff this afternoon and Sunday, give Veronica a preview Monday or Tuesday, depending, and still have time to incorporate her suggestions by Wednesday. Maybe start it at 11:00 a.m.?

Satisfied that I at least had something concrete to propose I picked up my cell phone, glanced at the time, and called the provost's office. Rufus should still be there if his assistant knew what she was talking about.

. . .

I checked carefully to make sure there wasn't a student lurking behind my car before I pulled out of the parking space. The university was trying to transform itself into a pedestrian campus by moving student parking farther and farther away from the heart of campus. It was working, in a way. Now students wandered across streets and parking lots seemingly confident that they wouldn't get run over. It made some drivers a little irate to find their path blocked by undergraduates wandering down the middle of the street chattering away on their cell phones or listening to their iPods, blissfully unaware of the line of cars behind them.

. . .

I got out of the car and had almost reached the door before I remembered the box Albert had given me. I turned around and went back to get it. I was going to have to get started on the memorial service video right away to be sure to have it ready for the service. Rufus wanted it over and done with. "To put that chapter in the university's history behind us," as he put it. I thought he was being way too generous. At best Sean was going to be a couple of pages, maybe only a paragraph or two. Of course, dying did give him some historical significance. But only as a novelty, I decided. Surely somebody else had died at a retirement party on campus. Or maybe not.

The memorial service was to be next Wednesday—a week to the day from the day he died—in the afternoon so people could go home after the service.

Rufus had been fine with having the ceremony on Wednesday but disagreed that eleven was a good time. "Too close to lunch. Around here, if you have it then people will expect to be fed afterward and, as the person this is in memory of got poisoned at a function in that very building, I'd say you'd better do it earlier or later." We'd settled on four o'clock. People wouldn't have to go back to work afterward, and those that wanted to could go have a drink together. He agreed to say a few words before the service, so I could blame the time on the provost in case Veronica or others wanted to do things differently.

I set the box down on the kitchen counter. "You know you're not supposed to be up here." The Black looked at me and yawned. He'd probably been napping there. "Go on," I pushed him a little. "Get off the counter." The insolent beast stood and stretched, leaning forward with one back leg outstretched behind him, parallel to the counter. Every time he stretched like that I remembered how he had eased himself out of the pet carrier when the lady from the humane society had brought him to his new home—his forever home she called it. He had come out slowly as if reluctant to give up the shelter of the known to enter the unknown. And he had kept on coming out until I realized I'd brought home a small panther. Having shown me that getting down from the counter was his idea, he soundlessly dropped to the floor.

All the while I could hear the sound of Tan's tail beating against the side of the house. She was standing at a right angle to the backdoor, so that if it had been raining she would have had some shelter because of the overhang. It wasn't raining, of course. But why risk it? I let her in and realized that while it wasn't time for her supper, it had been a long time since my breakfast.

After a late lunch I went down into my home office and got swallowed up by the project. Sometimes it happens that way. I came to in the early evening and got up to stretch. Movement on my part signaled to The Black that I was now alert enough to start attending to my primary responsibilities: The Black and, to a lesser extent, Tan. It was, he explained to me, time for supper.

I don't know why cats think that they are speeding up the process by winding between your legs as you're trying to walk. Maybe they think it's positive reinforcement? Anyway, if I'd wanted to do something besides feed them, I'd have stood a good chance of falling over my own feet—with a cat's help. It was Tan that was getting supper, her only meal of the day. The Black just got a treat because—well, if he didn't he'd be trying to eat Tan's food. And Tan would probably have let him. The Black had made it clear to the dog who was in charge of this household. Tan knew she wasn't anybody's boss. I was still making valiant attempts to convince the cat of my superiority as the human, but I could tell that he didn't fully believe it.

I had never told The Black that the Egyptians had once considered cats to be gods. He was arrogant enough. Maybe he already knew.

In a couple of minutes I put The Black's treat down and then Tan's supper. Once The Black was distracted Tan didn't have to defend her food bowl. I glanced at the clock and realized that the Friday night high school game was on so I turned on the radio and tuned to the local station, adjusted the volume so that it was more than background noise, but not much more. The announcers were local, but that didn't mean they were bad. One of the men had been doing the Friday games for so long that he was an institution.

A couple of years ago the radio station he'd been on had been bought up by one of those conglomerates that try to homogenize the stations so they all sound the same, from coast to coast. I guess the idea is to eliminate any but essential local staff, but that kills the local color as well. So they stopped carrying the County High School football games in the middle of the season. The story I heard was that the first night the game wasn't on the air happened to be the night when a few of our local businessmen had been out at their hunting lodge trying to tune in the game after a day of playing cards and drinking. Tommy-Oh was back on the air the following week at a different radio station and it looked like he'd be broadcasting County High football as long as he wanted to.

His last name was Branson or Brandon, something like that, but everybody called him Tommy-Oh because he used the word so much in describing what happened. Oh, that was a dandy of a kick! Oh, he's got a case of the fumbles tonight! Oh, he's doing his momma and daddy proud tonight! Oh, oh, he caught them napping!

Anyway, with Tommy-Oh in the background I started working in the kitchen. I planned on barbecuing tomorrow and I was out of sauce. My sauce is better if it sits overnight, so I thought I'd make a batch of that as well as tonight's supper. I had a sauce recipe that I sort of followed but it made only a cup or some such and I like to make it in quantity. So I sort of followed the recipe and sort of acted like a mad scientist. The combination usually worked pretty well.

I decided to take the country ribs out of the freezer and move them into the fridge. I wanted to make sure the pork was thawed by the time I went to put it in the smoker tomorrow. I'm careful cooking pork, but I hate to dry it out. I took the package of meat out of the freezer after pawing through the various blocks of ice for long enough to make my hands cold, put it on a plate, and stuck it in the fridge. I had to balance the plate on top of some jars, but it fit well enough.

Then I started pulling the ingredients out of the cupboard while wondering what I was going to cook for supper, keeping half an ear tuned to the radio. It was the beginning of the season and nobody was expecting much from County High this year. Last year's powerful senior class had graduated and this year's class just wasn't as gifted.

The guy who cuts my hair had a son who played football for County High and was on the varsity as a sophomore. I'd been hearing about what a quarterback the boy was going to be for years now. He started out the year as the backup and in the third quarter of their first game the starter got injured and Jason had to come in to finish the game. Anyway, Jason, the guy's son, lit up the field—couple of touchdown passes, some scrambling for first downs, and bingo, County High wins. He starts the next game and throws five touchdowns. So it turns out the guy who cuts my hair knows more than cutting hair. It was kind of fun.

I had all the jars and bottles for making the sauce spread out on the counter and started measuring. First the dry ingredients so I could mix them up and then add the liquids. I was quadrupling the amount, so I had to do some math while I was measuring. I can't say I was paying any attention to the radio, until Tommy-Oh went off.

"Oh, oh, oh, oh! That was pretty! I haven't seen one better in a loooong time, my friends. It was a fake pass play, folks, with a nice handoff to the tailback. I didn't see the quarterback hand off the ball and neither did the defense. We were all thinking pass until that tailback scooted by with the ball tucked under his arm. Got to keep your eye on the ball! Name of the game. Good gain before the defense realized who had the ball. This Jason Taylor is quite the magician—good sleight-of-hand. Now the defense sees it, now it doesn't!"

Tommy-Oh aficionados could tell by the inflection of his voice how impressive the play was, I had to go by my own rule of thumb—how many ohs he used. So that had been a four-oh play. I made a mental note to take back up trying to juggle. Probably a way to keep yourself mentally and physically sharp.

Got to keep your mind on the recipe, I reminded myself. Had I added the hot sauce or not? I turned the radio down a little more and stared at the bottle. It was on the right hand side of the pan. That should have meant that I'd picked the bottle up from the left where the unused spices and things were, added a few drops, then put it down on the right, but I'd let Tommy-Oh distract me. Keep your mind on what you're doing and your eye on the ball. I added a few drops more just in case and went on through the rest of the ingredients then stirred the concoction. I'd be able to tell after it had melded a little. I set the bowl on the stove so I could stir it occasionally while I was cooking supper.

I heard the crowd noise over the radio and knew something had happened, probably something good for the home team or the noise would have sounded more like a groan.

I moved the wok over to the stove. I'd been staring at video pretty much all afternoon and early evening and had some nervous energy to burn off. A little beef and broccoli stir-fry would be the right amount of chopping and cooking. I'd cooked it so often I didn't need the recipe or if I'd forgotten something, it didn't matter. Shoot, I might be adding things that weren't called for. There was some cooked white rice in the freezer that I could nuke and an open bottle of merlot.

I poured myself a scotch and turned the radio back up. It was time to relax.

CHAPTER 9
SATURDAY

Saturday seemed to drag. I got up and did my errands before the roads and stores filled up with game day traffic. Some people like to go out and mingle with the crowds, enjoying the bustle and hubbub, I suppose. I'm not one of them. I mentally kicked myself for not doing more of the errands yesterday. I'd retired but I hadn't retrained myself to take advantage of not being at work eight hours a day five days a week. Why shop at the same time the nonretirees of the world have to? The stores themselves wanted us to come in at different times of the week. That's why there were senior discounts on Tuesdays or Thursdays or whenever. And there ought not to be any discount at all during the evening rush hour. Don't get in the way of the poor working stiffs who were trying to pick something up on their way home from work!

It used to drive me crazy when I'd end up behind somebody who'd obviously just finally gotten around to shopping after a long day of who-knows-what. Mahjong? Bridge? Canasta? The cashier would tell them the total and then they'd get out their checkbook or wallet. Like it was a surprise that they had to pay! Of course, I'd gotten less irritated the older I got. Seeing the future, as it were.

Once back home I unpacked my purchases, put the groceries away, and put the special beer, Jamaican Red Stripe, in to chill. It had been an impulse purchase. I usually don't spend that much money on beer for me. But today I thought how good it would taste with the barbecue and, besides, it wasn't just for me. It was going to be a special evening.

It was a little early, but breakfast had been light and, anyway, I was hungry. I made a couple of sandwiches and sat down with the morning paper.

Afterward I changed into scruffy clothes and went out into the yard. I had chores I needed to attend to but first Tan had to play ball. The dog and I had lived alone together for a while before The Black had come into our lives and I think Tan missed the simpler times when it was just man and dog. Not that she didn't like the cat. Sometimes I thought they might be ganging up on me but that was when supper was late. And it was Tan's supper. I left dry food out for TB during the day so he could eat any time he wanted.

I started slow with short throws, trying to limber up my shoulder and wrist. Tan was all over the ball, dropping it at my feet and then racing out to where I'd been throwing it to spin around and face me, tail going ninety to nothing. She looked like a shortstop waiting for somebody to hit the ball to her. I bounced a few in front of her so she could catch them on the hop, then threw long a couple of times. We were through when she didn't bring it back, just got it and then lay down, panting. It used to take longer before she was willing to quit.

I started cleaning up the patio, clearing off the leaves and dusting off the table and chairs. Not that it would keep, of course. It's impossible to keep the outdoors clean and tidy. The screen porch was in good shape. In the spring, the pollen drifts in and turns all the surfaces a hideous shade of green, but it stayed pretty clean the rest of the year.

I went to check the grill and decided that it could do with a little cleaning. It lives on the screen porch up against the chimney—the other side of the fireplace—so I can grill rain or shine, but I roll it outside to clean it. A friend had given me a grill scrubber that appeared to be a pumice stone on a stick, only fancier. Turned out what looked like stone was "recycled ingredients" and the directions "strongly" suggested wiping off any dust that was left on the grates "after use." Since I normally just give the grates a swipe or two with a wire brush or tinfoil before starting the fire, I'd hesitated to try it until I had time to do something about the dust. Today, I decided, I had time.

The stone did well on the flat surfaces of the grates but didn't get into the grooves, which was OK. I figured that the meat would be less likely to stick on the surface and left it at that. I was sure that once I got the grill hot enough whatever lurked in the grooves was just going to add to the flavor. I pulled the grates out and took them over to the spigot to rinse them off. A better idea, I thought, than trying to "wipe the dust off" regardless of what the instructions had said. Now all I had to do was fire up the grill to dry the grates and sanitize whatever was left on them. That's one of the reasons I like gas grills. Catch somebody building a charcoal fire just to dry the grates.

It was too early to put the meat on. I liked to cook the pork slow with some wood chips for a smoky flavor, but I wasn't one of those purists that had to slow cook for days at a time. I found with the cuts I used that a couple of hours worked just fine, and cooking that slow meant you didn't have to hover over the food worrying about flare-ups. Which was another thing I liked about this grill in particular—a good design that minimized, if it didn't quite eliminate, flare-ups.

Come to think on it, I guess that was another thing I liked about gas grills in general. I grill year-round, replacing parts as I go until I can't repair the grill anymore and have to buy a new one. And every time I go looking for what I'd bought before, they don't make it anymore. Char-Broil, Weber, Grillmaster, or whoever has changed the design, added features, turbocharged it, or made it more aerodynamic. I don't know.

Lava rocks were in, then they were out. Ceramic briquettes were better, then they weren't. Windows in the lids so you could see if what you were cooking was on fire, if you could see through the windows at all. Thermometers built into the cover that did you no good when you didn't close the cover. Thermometers that registered how hot the burners were at a particular spot. Side burners! Trust me, I make my grills last as long as I can and, as a result, whenever I go out to buy one I get stunned by the new features. And, I might add, the price. Still, it was a heck of a lot cheaper than buying a new car and you got the same feeling.

But charcoal grills all look the same as last year's model. A metal box to build a fire in. The thought struck me. Did grill manufacturers know something about people that the rest of us didn't? Do cooks who use gas want different models and features while traditionalists stay with charcoal, lighter fluid, and the same type grill? Could you predict a man's politics by the grill he used? I tried to match up known grill preferences with bumper stickers but had too small a sample. But it was a working hypothesis that needed further testing. How should I go about collecting more data?

I finished with the patio, put the grill back in place, and still had a little time to kill before the game started. What next? I scratched my chin and realized that it scratched back. That's right. I'd decided to shower and shave after I'd run errands and cleaned up the yard. All of a sudden, I'd gone from plenty of time to running short of time. Happens to me all the time.

. . .

Clean shaven, with my hair still damp, wearing a clean pair of jeans, sneakers, and a nice knit shirt I was ready to receive guests but still had a few things I needed to do.

I entered the kitchen and found myself with an audience. Tan and The Black were sitting staring up at me. "Supper? It's a little early isn't it?" The Black disagreed strongly and vocally and began to fuss. Tan just perked up her ears hopefully and wagged her tail against the floor. I relented and fed Tan her supper and put out a treat for TB. "There," I said, "are you two satisfied?" and turned to the stove.

The BBQ sauce had sat in the fridge for twenty-four hours and all the flavors had had time to meld. I stirred the sauce, scooping bay leaves and lemon slices out as they surfaced. Once I'd found all of them, I crossed over to the sink and tossed them down the drain and turned on the garbage disposal. Grinding up lemon slices adds a nice clean smell to the air. Back at the stove, I turned on the burner beneath the sauce pan and adjusted it to low. I wanted to warm it up before adding the butter.

Speaking of warming, I'd meant to take the meat out earlier to let it come up to room temperature. I turned back to the fridge just as Tan started barking excitedly at the door, her tail just a blur of movement.

The door opened and Bobby stuck her head in the room. "Safe to come in?"

"You ought to know that Tan's just saying hello. Come on in." I started toward the door a little embarrassed at not realizing she'd arrived. I'd been looking forward to her visit and had been trying to keep an eye out for her arrival.

She opened the door the rest of the way and I could see that she was wearing a black blouse with scooped neckline, black jeans, matching shoes, silver bracelets and earrings that matched the silver of her hair. She looked wonderful. She took a breath and then stepped inside.

It was at that instant that I realized she was carrying an overnight bag. Our eyes met. She lifted the bag and, with no pretense, said in that husky voice of hers, "Should I put this in the guest room?"

I could feel my heart pound. We were both old enough not to play games and knew, or thought we knew, that the other was attracted, but she had cut through it all with a startling directness that was her.

"Hell, any room in the house that appeals to you." My voice croaked and I could feel my face turning red. "Just don't put it back in the car."

"It's not the house that appeals to me." Her grin was wicked. She set the bag on the floor and closed the door behind her. "But, all of a sudden, I could use a drink."

"Excellent idea! Dirty martini or wine?"

"Do you have Grey Goose?"

"I do indeed." A certain tension between us had disappeared only to be replaced with a different tension and anticipation.

I had started keeping the vodka in the freezer when I found out how cold she liked her drinks. I got the shaker out of the liquor cabinet, olives and vermouth from the fridge, and the vodka out of the freezer. On second thought, I didn't need the vermouth.

"One Grey Goose martini, extra dirty, three olives, and as dry as the Sahara." Bobby had followed me into the kitchen and now stood at the counter. I put the drink down in front of her. I could see tiny flecks of ice sparkling on the surface of the liquid. "Please note that I do not say 'Sahara desert.'"

She smiled and took a sip lifting the almost overfull glass by the stem. "So noted. With approval. Mmmmm. And speaking of approval, this is just the way I like it. Nobody makes a better Grey Goose than you do, Crawford."

"Why, thank you ma'am, but, not to be pedantic, a 'Grey Goose' is a brand of liquor, not a drink like a Manhattan or Tom Collins or Rob Roy. I walked back to the liquor cabinet to mix myself a drink, if you want to call pouring scotch over ice "mixing a drink." I grabbed the Cluny, hesitated, dumped the cubes into the sink and then reached for a different bottle and poured myself a double—no rocks. It was an insult to put this scotch on ice.

"Of course it is," she said serenely. "What are you drinking? That's not your usual scotch."

"No," I grinned. "It's a single malt scotch that I save for very special occasions. Very special." I walked around the counter and pointed toward the den. "Shall we sit?"

Bobby picked up her drink and followed me into the den. She picked the overstuffed armchair to sit in and promptly shucked her shoes and curled her feet under her. She swore she was comfortable. I sat down in a cane-bottomed rocking chair across from her. One of my favorite rockers. A young cousin had once told me that he'd never been in a house that had more rocking chairs. I took it as a compliment, as indeed he had meant it to be.

"'Of course it is'? By what circuitous path did you reach that conclusion?"

"I like martinis. I like them made a certain way—always with Grey Goose. Hence," her voice took on a faint hint of academia, "by association, a martini made to my specifications can

be called a Grey Goose. Like saying 'the sails' move across the
sea when what you really mean is 'the ships.'"

I took a small sip of some of the best scotch it's been my
pleasure to drink. "I never refer to 'the sails' when I mean 'the
ships.'"

"Idiot."

The insult actually sounded pretty good to me when she said
it. I wondered if I was losing my objectivity.

"Of course you don't, but writers do. Poets in particular.
There's a term for it. It's a figure of speech." She chewed gently
on her bottom lip. I could see the wheels spinning as she tried to
conjure up the elusive word.

"Oh, right." Something from a Latin class in high school
stirred briefly in my memory. "Yes, I do know of what you
speak. But I don't now know, if I ever did know, the term for
that particular figure of speech." I did know that Bobby was certainly easy to look at. I liked the way her curls outlined her face.

"Synecdoche!"

"Schenectady?"

"Se-nek-de-kee. That's it. Either a part referring to the whole
or, if memory serves, the whole referring to a part."

I raised my glass toward her. "I sit corrected. To synecdoche—and your Grey Gooses. Grey Geese?"

She leaned forward toward me holding out her glass until she
could clink hers on mine. "To synecdoche."

. . .

I wondered how long we'd both been silent and if we'd reached
the point in our relationship where we could be comfortable with
silence. "So . . . Bobby a nickname?" I asked carefully. "Your

full name is . . ." I had a feeling there was a story there. I didn't want to push too soon but I didn't want her to think I wasn't interested.

"That Bobby is short for?" She raised her eyebrows questioningly.

"Yeah," I threw caution to the winds. "And why spell it with a *y*?"

"It's short for Barbara. And I wasn't going to be a Barbie." She shook her head hard enough to make her curls bounce then settle back in place. "Thanks, Mattel. Messed that name up for several generations of children. And Barb, while appropriate in some ways," she grinned, "was always going to be made into Barbie."

"Oh." I felt relieved. Neither too soon nor too late.

"I used Bobbie with an *ie* at first, but I never drew a heart for the dot over the *i*. Then, in June 1968 I decided to spell it the way he had. Kind of in memory."

"The summer of 1968?" I knew damn well what she was talking about. "You must have been—what twelve or thirteen?" I'd been eighteen.

"I was in love with him." Her eyes moistened. "And they killed him."

"Yeah." I remembered waking up to hear that Robert Kennedy had been assassinated. That was the summer the world got a little dimmer and dirtier in my eyes.

"So," I said trying to lighten both our moods, "named after a U.S. attorney general, are you?" She was nice enough to laugh at the feeble joke. She's got a nice laugh.

Sunday morning was quiet. Bobby had left and I was at the kitchen counter drinking coffee and reading the sports section, slowly coming up to speed. Somehow we'd never gotten around to turning on the game. There had been too much to say—and do. The evening had been full, momentous even, and there were lots of things to think about. I ran my finger around the lip of the mug. There was time to enjoy life as it now stood. I was aware of what had changed and that the future could bring both good and bad. But right now I was just being comfortable in the present.

"Isn't that right, Tan?" The dog was lying by the door and perked up at the sound of her name. Her tail began to thump against the tile floor. "Even when our head is in the clouds, we still need to take time to smell the roses, no—walk the dog, right?"

Hearing the word "walk" was enough to set Tan off. She started bouncing up and down and barking. I walked over to the door and took her lead off the hook. "Sit," I said and she did sit, but she was vibrating from her excitement so much that it was hard to slip the choke collar over her head. Hard, but not impossible. I got down on one knee and finally got it on her. I didn't connect the lead to the collar. Tan and I can walk together without her being on the lead. But there was a jerk who had just moved into the subdivision who thought he didn't need to use a lead with his dogs either.

He was mistaken.

To top it off, he sometimes just let them out on their own to terrorize the neighbors. Anyway, it's hard to have animal control respond to your complaint about unleashed dogs while you're standing there with a dog that's not on a lead. Tan and I walk with a lead and a cell phone nowadays.

I stood up. "Don't act like we haven't gone for a walk in weeks!" I don't know why I bother. She would act the same way if we just got back from a walk and I decided to turn around and go back out again.

"Sit. Stay." Tan sat and I opened the door. She was still vibrating, but she was waiting for me to give her a command. "Release," I said and Tan burst through the open door and started sniffing the concrete carport. I closed the door behind us and followed Tan down the driveway.

. . .

I tried to bring my mind to bear on the day. I had more work to do on the video before Monday. I needed to get it into shape so that I could go in to campus and meet with Voni and Albert. I was pretty sure they would want to see what the memorial service looked like and I wanted to see how it worked with multiple projectors and a virtual wall. I knew how I thought it would work, but that's not always how something does work. If all the projectors weren't high-def, for instance, I'd have to change the sequencing. Move the older pictures onto those screens and . . .

The walk worked. I was able to focus on what I needed to think about. I looked up to see that we'd made the circuit and were back at the house. I stopped walking and Tan sat at my side. "Good dog!" I said and reached down to pat her. If we worked at it she would have been marvelously trained. Shoot, if she'd been able to read the training book, she'd have trained herself and me as well. If I was trainable, which remains to be seen.

We entered the house, Tan on her way to her water bowl and me to the coffee pot. I freshened up the cup, took a sip, and noticed that the light on the phone was blinking. I had a voice mail message.

At first I thought it was Bobby and my heart jumped. It wasn't her number, but my reaction made me decide to call her later, after I listened to the voice mail. What was Provost Rufus George doing calling me on a Sunday? I put it on speaker phone and grabbed a pencil and pad of paper.

"James," I would have recognized the courtly southern accent immediately even if caller ID hadn't told me it was from the provost's office. "This is Rufus George. I hope I haven't caught you at a bad time." Rufus stopped to chuckle. "I don't see how I could have since I haven't really caught you at all, just your answering service." He cleared his voice and went on. "You may not have heard the tragic news. Albert Worthy died late Friday night or early Saturday." Rufus paused, gave a little sigh and went on. "The police believe it was either suicide or an accident.

"I know that you're working on Dr. Thomas's memorial video and I hope this won't interfere with your work schedule. I'm a little concerned about an issue and I'd like to get your opinion on it, if you would be so kind. When you get this message, if it's not too late, could you join me for a late Sunday dinner at the University Club? I'll save a seat for you."

I just stared at the phone as the voice of the machine went on about how I could delete, save, archive, forward, and so on the message. Being in a state of shock, I opted to save the message.

It was shocking enough to hear that Albert was dead, what was it? Two days after Sean died? But it was almost mind-numbing for Rufus to have called me with the information. When you throw in the facts that it was Sunday morning; he called from his office; and he wanted to meet over Sunday dinner at the University Club—I realized that it wasn't almost mind-numbing. It *was* mind numbing.

I had known Rufus ever since his son, Jon, and I were in Cub Scouts together. Lord, what a long time ago that was. Jon broke the George family connection to the university and went off to college, so we saw less and less of each other, but Rufus never forgot he knew me even though at the university the gap between provost and multimedia hack was pretty significant.

Rufus had been a part of the university for so long everybody knew him. His family had been linked to the university for generations and he was the last of that link and the last of his kind. He was universally loved and respected. Well, universally enough. He was a fair man and had an inclination to be kindly, but there was steel underneath. He couldn't have gotten to be provost and been such a good one otherwise.

My brain began to thaw. Rufus had probably gone to early morning church service and then into his office. Dinner was the noon meal for all southerners of a certain age or older. Lots of people went to the University Club on Sunday after church services.

OK, so I could explain to myself the circumstances surrounding the invitation. What I couldn't get my mind around was the "issue" he was concerned about. What the hell did Rufus George want my "opinion" about?

There were tales on campus of how Rufus seemed to sense things. Sometimes it was spooky how much he knew. This might be one of those times.

I glanced over at the kitchen clock and realized that confused and dazed as I was, I had better hurry if I wasn't going to keep him waiting.

. . .

I arrived at the University Club with my driving record intact, no
students killed, maimed, or suffering from accident-induced
long-term trauma. Surprisingly there was a space under one of
the grand old oak trees so I was able to park in the shade. This
was a time to forget the sunshield. The Club was housed in an
antebellum mansion that had undergone extensive and repeated
renovation. The quality of the food had gone through its own
series of pendulum swings, from the legendary meals of the past
to the steam-table buffets of cafeteria-quality food to the current
small renaissance, or so I'd heard. I didn't frequent the place.

I entered through the twelve-foot doors and speculated on
how much heat or air conditioning escaped every time somebody
came in the door. I noticed the Please Wait to Be Seated sign
and wondered how long that had been in force or if it had always
been there. I had recovered from the shock of Rufus's call and
was in a questioning frame of mind. Then I saw the hostess.

She looked up at me serenely and asked, "Are you meeting
someone?"

She, I assure you, had not been there the last time I went to
the Club. Indeed, up until that very moment, I had never been
interested in being a member of the Club, although university
employees were encouraged to join. I had never seen the attrac-
tion. As I said, up until then.

She was beautiful. Hair a light red or reddish blonde, eyes
brilliant blue, skin flawless. Her basic black dress fit her well,
snug but not tight. She was trim and shapely and her smile was
warm and friendly. She was young, but it wasn't the beauty of
youth. She would age into a spectacular looking woman. I was

dumbstruck. She had known that I wasn't a member and that indicated there were smarts to go with those looks. I recognized that fact but was still trying to figure out how to speak in front of such beauty.

She took pity on me. She must have been used to it. Grown men had probably become speechless at the sight of her for most of her life. To give her credit she didn't act like she knew she was incredibly beautiful.

"The provost said that a Mr. Crawford might join him for dinner?" She raised her flawless eyebrows questioningly.

Her voice was as good as her looks. I stared for another second and then croaked. "Right. Crawford. That's me." I hooked my thumb back at my chest and croaked. "James Crawford. Rufus expecting me." I realized that I sounded like Tarzan in the old movies.

"Pleased to meet you, Mr. Crawford, my name is Stephanie. Now, if you'll follow me." She turned and walked toward the dining rooms. I was glad she hadn't asked me to "walk this way." It was physically impossible.

"You can just point me in the right direction." The words came out fine this time.

"Do you know the Club well?" She sounded like she didn't think I did. "It's filled with nooks and crannies and on Sundays we use them all. I must confess that it took me a while to figure out where all the rooms are. Why even the waitstaff get lost sometimes."

I silently surrendered and followed her through two rooms filled with diners, some of whom looked vaguely familiar, then down a hallway and through a doorway I didn't know existed that opened onto a small room with only two tables. One was empty and the other held Provost George.

"Here he is," said Stephanie sweetly. Rufus folded his napkin, wiped his lips, and stood. "You described him perfectly, Uncle Rufus. I recognized him right away even if he looks younger than you said."

"Thank you, Stephanie. I knew I could depend on you. It's hard when you're my age to judge age." Rufus smiled at her in a decidedly avuncular manner. Then he reached across the table to shake my hand. "James, thanks for coming." He nodded toward Stephanie. "God-daughter," he answered the unasked question that must have been in my eyes. "I'm an old friend of the family."

"It's always a pleasure to see you, Rufus." I bowed in Stephanie's direction. "And a pleasure and a privilege to meet Miss Stephanie."

She smiled and nodded her head. "And to meet you as well." She looked at Rufus's plate. "Are you interested in a full meal, Mr. Crawford? Or something lighter?" Rufus had said "dinner" in the southern fashion and, clearly, had meant it.

"Lighter. If I have a hearty meal at noon I have to go home and nap and I can't do that today." I turned back to Rufus. "Go ahead and eat, Rufus. It'll get cold or warm, depending."

"A cup of soup and a sandwich?" asked Stephanie brightly. "The special today is gazpacho and a grilled cheese sandwich. Four cheeses, actually, on whole wheat. If you like gazpacho, this one is special."

"That would be perfect. Thanks, Stephanie."

"I'll put the order in for you then. Now, if there's nothing else?" She looked at Rufus and then me. "Good day, gentlemen." And she left the room.

I looked at Rufus noting that he hadn't sat back down, not to mention started eating again. "That is one very attractive young lady."

"She takes after her mother." He pointed at the table. "Shall we?"

He started to eat, but not before he'd asked me how I was enjoying early retirement with the emphasis on "early." I chattered a little on the many plusses of retirement while he nodded or looked inquiringly at me. Every once in a while I would run down and he would stop eating and toss out another topic for us to discuss. I had begun to wonder where my lunch was when the waitress came in with my soup and sandwich. After I had assured her that a glass of water was all I wanted to drink and that everything else was fine, Rufus spoke up. "Velma, you can take my plate, if you will."

Velma, and that was the name on her tag, you never know who Rufus might know, left my side and went around the table to pick up the plate. "Mr. Rufus, you feeling OK? Why you didn't even finish your spoon bread." Yes, I'd say that she'd been working at the Club for years.

Rufus wiped his lips with his napkin, folded it, and put it on the table. "Nevertheless, I'm finished. Thank you, Velma. No reflection on the food, just the nature of the day. Give my compliments to the chef. By the way, would you close the door after you? We don't want to be disturbed."

Snookered, I thought. I looked down at the soup and sandwich and realized I was trapped. Well, I couldn't pay for the food. I wasn't a member of the Club. But I guessed I would pay. Rufus was after something.

"James, I hope you'll go ahead and eat. Please excuse me for talking about business, as it were, while you're eating, but I have something I need to say to you and then something I need to ask you. And please wait until I'm through before you respond." He cocked his head inquiringly at me.

I was wrong again. Rufus George wanted to tell me something and that's what was going to happen. I certainly wasn't going to stop him. "Please go right ahead, Rufus. The floor is yours." I picked up my spoon and took a small mouthful of soup. Stephanie was right. It was delicious.

Rufus put the tips of his fingers together almost as if to pray and touched his index fingers to his lips. "I believe," he dropped his hands to the table and his eyes followed them, "that I made a serious mistake and that the university and you, in particular, have suffered because of it."

He lifted his eyes and met mine as I sat frozen, soup spoon in hand staring back at him. "Rufus, as many things right that you've done—"

He held up the palm of his hand toward me. "Everybody makes mistakes, James. I know that." A small smile slipped across his face. "Few know it better since I'm older than most. Mistakes are a part of life that we try to learn from.

"What I'm very much afraid is that I made this mistake worse, much, much worse, by thinking I could fix it. Thinking that with just a little push I could make things come out all right." He sat still for a few heartbeats. "I've learned to live with making mistakes, but this is different. And, ironically, I need you, one of the ones who suffered the most from my mistake, to help me make the best of it. James Crawford," I felt the hairs on the back of my neck start to rise, "I need your help."

I took my time driving home from the University Club. Rufus had given me a lot to think about and some hard decisions to make. I'm not saying that I was driving while impaired, mind you, just a little distracted.

Thinking about Rufus and Sean I was struck by the difference between them. One cared about how to make the world better while the other cared about making himself look better. Like the difference between gold and glitter. There was more to it than that, of course. Neither man was shallow. No, that isn't right. Sean was shallow. But he frothed the water so that it looked like there were some depths there—or might be. Rufus's depths were real. Deep, still water, no froth there.

Tan was bouncing up and down behind the fence as I pulled into the driveway. She had adjusted to my early retirement faster than anyone else. I walked into the house and dropped my keys, wallet, and phone into the bowl where they lived. The Black was sitting on the counter staring straight at me, eyes unblinking. OK, the cat hadn't exactly adjusted to me being home all the time. He took it as his due. I should be around to do his bidding.

"You're right," I said to the cat. "We need to talk."

. . .

Albert had died from strangulation. The police had found him in his downtown loft apartment hanging from an exposed beam. The rope was made of silk—a kind often used in erotic practices including but not limited to bondage and self-strangulation. I felt a little squeamish hearing about it but Rufus never flinched, reciting the details calmly and succinctly. The police were inclined to believe that it was an accident rather than a suicide. He hadn't left a note and the possibility of a fatal mistake is part of the thrill of self-strangulation.

I sat still as Rufus talked, a forgotten sandwich in one hand either on its way to or from my mouth—which was closed, thank goodness. At least my involuntary response wasn't to sit there slack-jawed and drooling. The fact that Albert had been homosexual didn't surprise me much, I guess. He kept his sexual orientation to himself like most of us at the computer center—we were professionals and behaved like it—mostly. Upon reflection, there had been a woman who was something of a proselytizer.

The surprise was that Rufus knew—had known it. It was a fact he provided matter-of-factly. The police might suspect, but nowadays were careful to keep such opinions to themselves. As he talked I began to see the outline fall into place. Albert had left his partner in Shannons, Mississippi, when he'd accepted Sean's job offer. The partner, as it turned out, had refused to move with him to Shelbyville having grown up here—a child of a very prominent family. So prominent that I was sure I could put a name to them even though Rufus was being careful to leave everybody anonymous with the exception of the deceased.

If it was the family I thought it had to be, it was the patriarch who didn't want the fact that one of his descendants was gay to be common knowledge—if, indeed, he knew. The old man said loudly and often that he'd rather see a child of his in a coffin than with a drink in his hands. I could just imagine how thrilled he'd be to see one holding another man's hand. The more I thought about it the more I believed that the rest of the family must be keeping it from the man who controlled the family fortune.

The partner had heard of Albert's death and was crushed. Albert had not wanted to leave Shannons, Mississippi, or his partner. He had been happy there. Sean Thomas had forced Albert to leave by means that the partner was a little vague about. Still, I found that part of the story easy to believe. Sean had needed Albert's management skills, and what Sean wanted he got.

Albert had called the partner after Sean died of food poisoning and was grieved at the loss but, at the same time, saw it as a release. He would be able to return to Shannons—his position there had not been filled—and to his partner. But something about Sean's death worried him. He hadn't told his partner what it was—just that something didn't seem right.

To Albert's partner it all added up. Albert had not committed suicide. As far as self-strangulation was concerned, Albert was terrified of ropes and nooses—the thought that Albert would have owned a silk rope, much less used it was absolutely ridiculous—out of the question. He wouldn't have done either of those things. The partner had figured it out.

Albert Worthy had been murdered by person or persons unknown.

He had been murdered and the police were covering it up. The partner was so sure about this that he was going to return to Shelbyville, reveal his relationship with Albert, explain that Albert had been killed, and demand justice. He had sworn to do just that even though the publicity would cause his family and himself great suffering—unless.

Unless—we were just talking theoretically—unless somebody else would step forward and prove that Albert had been murdered—or the unthinkable had happened. Someone who could be trusted to keep the sordid details in the background as

much as possible while figuring out what had happened. Someone other than the police. Somebody who could investigate on
behalf of the university and the partner's family. Someone who
was recently retired and needed something to do.

It wasn't clear to me at what point Rufus stopped presenting
the partner's point of view and moved on to the family's. And
how the distress that this publicity would cause the family could
translate into actual harm to the university and by extension
harm to the university family, which included everyone in this
room—all two of us—and how somebody could keep all that
from happening.

And how Rufus believed that somebody was me.

. . .

I went to the door to let Tan in while The Black snaked around
my ankles. Tan bounded into the room wagging her tail so hard
that she formed a comma. Around suppertime my animals become very affectionate.

While I was feeding the animals, I realized that the soup and
sandwich at the University Club had been some time ago and
now I was interested in something a little more substantial.

I walked over to the refrigerator and stared at it. Sometimes
when I wanted to think something out, I'd cook a dish that required a little mindless chopping or stirring, something that oc-
cupied the hands and let my mind wander. A salad, I decided,
opened the door and realized that I hadn't bought any lettuce the
last time I had gone to the grocery store. No problem as far as
the staples were concerned, but the lettuce looked more than sad.
Plan B, I thought. Time to thaw something out. I closed the refrigerator door, took the double boiler out of the drawer, added

water to the pan, and put it on the stove. Spaghetti meat sauce. I can't prepare spaghetti sauce for one. I have to make it in quantity, so I do and freeze the excess for times just like this.

I pulled one of the containers out of the freezer and stuck it in the microwave to start thawing. Let's see, three minutes at defrost? I just wanted to thaw it enough to get it out. I opened a cabinet and took down a red wine glass. I'd want red with supper so I might as well start there. I had bought a nice shiraz that should do fine. I wandered over to the wine rack and pulled the bottle out, cut the foil, opened it, and poured myself a glass. I swirled the wine and then held the glass up to the light. It had good legs.

When I was branching out from Mateus and lambrusco to other wines, with the help of some friends, we would pass on bits of information that we'd garnered from others who might have been further along in the process. One such was the importance of "legs" in red wines. I've since learned better. Wine with legs merely has a higher alcohol content than wine without legs. But I enjoy looking at wine in a glass made for it, so I still swirl the wine and look at the legs. For a moment I remembered Tom, Anna, Eleanor, and me holding up our glasses and trying to find the "legs" we'd heard about. That was so many years ago.

By that time the microwave had beeped. I reached in and felt the plastic container. Still hard as a rock, so three minutes more. Punched some numbers and pushed start. Reached into the freezer and pulled a couple of slices of sourdough bread out to put in the toaster oven. I would cook the pasta in the water that was heating in the bottom of the double boiler. I always do. Angel hair, because that's what was on hand, but that works, thick sauce, thin pasta. Maybe some garlic butter on the bread? I'd deal with that after the sauce got hot.

Satisfied with the supper plan, I sat down at the counter and sipped the wine. Very nice, I thought. I'll have to thank the woman at Wines 4 U. What was her name? Jennifer?

. . .

It had shocked me to find out how much Rufus knew about me. Not that I'd tried to hide any of it. That part about being a "trained investigator"? I'd joined the U.S. Navy—well, the Navy Reserve for the extra money, that's how that got started. The university had, historically, never paid that well. Never paid staff that well, I should say. Administrators and faculty, they operated under different rules. But the university was patriotic. People in the Reserves got paid their salary while they were on active duty. And it didn't count against vacation. From my point of view they were paying me to serve and so was Uncle Sam.

The Shore Patrol had a minimum height requirement that I just met. There were policemen in the Reserve unit too. Shelbyville didn't overpay them either. So I had gotten to know them, drilled with them, was even friends with some. I never thought much about it. But Rufus had. Thought enough about it that he considered it as "one of the resources" I would bring with me as a "trained investigator."

Well, I'd have to give him that. I'd listened to the stories about real police work at drill. I'd taken the courses and training the Navy offered, just to get the promotions that raised the pay grade. But Rufus had put his own spin on it.

I picked up the wine glass and took another sip then got up, took the container of sauce out of the microwave, and was able

to pop the still-frozen contents out and put them into the top of
the double boiler. I put the cover on and went back to the wine.

Yes, Rufus could tell that he had shocked me. Wouldn't let
me give him an answer until I'd had time to think it over. He'd
offered to give me the names of the partner and his family but
I'd told him to wait. His instincts had been right. I needed to decide this regardless of who was involved. Besides I was pretty
sure I could figure out who they were if I wanted to. He'd smiled
at that comment as if it proved his point. I wanted to think it
over—or mull it over, as I seemed to be doing. The man had
asked me for a favor. Could I turn him down just because I
wasn't sure that I was qualified? Or even wanted to be qualified?

. . .

I was standing in the kitchen drumming my fingers on the counter wondering what I should do when the phone rang. I glanced
at the caller ID and wondered why Rufus was calling. I thought
he'd made his case and wouldn't jostle my elbow while I was
struggling with my decision. Then I took a closer look at the
phone number—it was out of state.

"Jon?" He'd been named after his father but, growing up,
they called him by his middle name. There was no "Big Rufus"
and "Little Rufus" in the George household.

"Hey, Ford. It's been a long time."

He was right. I hadn't spoken to the provost's son in years.
He went by Rufus now and, for that matter, not many called me
Ford. Names of our childhood—sometimes we grow out of
them, or deliberately put them aside—and then, out of nowhere,
they pop back up—reminders of what had been.

"At first I thought it was your dad calling me back. You know, caller ID. I was just talking to him earlier."

"I know." Jon paused and I could hear him take a deep breath. "I know what he talked to you about. That's why I've called. What he told you about Albert Worthy was the absolute truth." He sighed, then chuckled, "Cross my heart and hope to die, it's the truth. Albert Worthy never put a rope around his neck—never in a million years."

. . .

"Mmrrrpht?"

I was staring at the phone, had been since I hung up after talking to Jon. I glanced down to see The Black sitting by my feet looking up at me. His green eyes contrasted sharply with the black fur.

"Yes?" I said politely. "I'm still trying to think it through. Is that all right with you?" It seems to me that most people are polite when they talk to their pets. Or maybe it's just the pet owners I know. Anyway, we all talk to them.

The Black seemed to be considering what I'd said, then jumped up into my lap. Since I was sitting on a bar stool at the kitchen counter there wasn't as much lap available as there would have been, say, when I was sitting in my recliner. Nevertheless he nailed it, a nice gentle landing with no need for claws, the absence of which I was grateful for. He settled down immediately and I could feel him start to purr.

"What brought that on?" I asked. "Do you think the old man is in need of moral support?" I could feel the purring intensify.

Amused, I looked over at Tan who had settled down on her dog bed and had picked up an old rawhide bone that she'd been chewing on when she thought about it, off and on, for a couple of weeks. "How about you, Tan?" Not to be outdone, she thumped her tail against the floor.

"Well, I'm glad to know all the animals are behind me with that 'can do' spirit." I picked The Black up and poured him out onto the floor. "You're too heavy. You cut the circulation off to my legs."

TB walked over to Tan's bed and sat down facing me. OK, the pets were in agreement. That left me alone in my quandary. I thought again about all Rufus had said this afternoon and added what Jon had told me.

Mentally I could feel all the pieces fall into place. It wasn't going to be easy, but I wouldn't have hesitated if it was an easy thing he asked of me. I picked up the kitchen phone and took the business card out of my shirt pocket, glancing at it as I dialed. It rang twice and a woman answered. "Mrs. George?" I asked. "This is James Crawford. Is the provost in?"

"I believe he is, for you, James." I recognized her voice from years ago. That Virginia accent was quite distinctive. "He said he hoped you would call."

I heard the sound of a second phone being picked up. "James? Have you reached a decision so soon?" We both heard his wife discretely hang up the phone. "There's no reason for you to hurry."

"It's all right, Rufus. I've decided. I'll do it." I spoke the next part slowly and clearly so that both of us would know what I was committing myself to.

"I will investigate Albert Worthy's death. I will do what I can to find out if Albert was murdered."

There was a pause on the other end of the line, then Rufus spoke in his soft, southern tones, "James Crawford, I thank you.

You know I've made mistakes before, but this is not one of them. I know you'll do your best."

We said a few more words and then I put the phone down and exhaled deeply. Rufus had gotten what he had asked for. We would iron out any details tomorrow. I glanced at the wine glass and thought better of it. I got up and poured myself two fingers of single malt scotch, Macallan, into a short squat glass. Gave the meat sauce a quick stir while sipping my drink. The sauce had thawed and now was hot and bubbling. Satisfied, I took the top pan off and put it on a back burner that I turned on, but just barely. I turned up the heat for the water, to bring it to a full boil. I went to the pantry for the angel hair, came back and stared at the pot. Now, I thought to myself, I had to find a way to back those words up.

. . .

It turns out the old saying is wrong. A watched pot does boil. I realized the water was boiling and dropped in what I thought was the right amount of pasta. It was bound to be too much. I always cooked too much, but I preferred too much to not enough. I stirred the water and then got the butter and a jar of minced garlic out of the fridge. Cut an inch of butter off the stick and dropped it into a small bowl. Stuck the bowl in the micro-wave and nuked it for fifteen seconds at half power then took it out and began to mash it. The butter was still too hard so I nuked it a little longer still trying to keep from melting it entirely. All the while I kept an eye on the pasta to keep from overcooking it.

The butter was soft enough that I could now mix it with the minced garlic and spread it on the slices of bread. I put the bread on the tray in the toaster oven and turned it to broil. The pasta was done by then and I poured the water and pasta mix into a colander in the sink, shook the colander a couple of times and then dumped the pasta back into the pan, added a little olive oil and swirled the pasta around. Yep, I'd cooked too much. Fortunately Tan doesn't mind leftover pasta. She'd prefer it with the meat sauce but then, so do I.

I moved most of the pasta into a bowl, poured the meat sauce over it, and sprinkled Parmesan cheese over that. I took the bowl to the counter and put it at my place next to the wine glass. Somewhere along the way the Macallan had disappeared. I went back to the toaster oven, popped it open and slid the bread out onto a plate. A salad would have been nice, I thought, but this was good enough. A comfort meal Eleanor and I had called it.

I sat down to eat and thought to myself, a professional detective would probably start by looking for evidence.

And so I would too, first thing tomorrow.

It's hard to be totally self-absorbed when you've got pets. Maybe some people can do it, but not most of us. There I was staring up at the ceiling with my mind spinning around like one of those gerbils in an exercise wheel. Or so I imagined. Never having had a gerbil or been one, I might be mistaken. Anyway Tan was standing in the doorway of the bedroom softly panting. She'd been there for a while. Long enough to penetrate my consciousness. "OK, OK. I'll let you out, if that's what you want." I sat up on the edge of the bed my feet searching the floor for my slippers. Tan walked over and put her head on my knee and looked up into my face. I'm a sucker for brown eyes—big, adoring, moist—in dogs anyway.

"So, walk?" As soon as I'd said the word, I regretted it. Tan bolted from the room and raced to the front door thinking, I suppose, that I was right behind her. When she got there she found to her surprise that I wasn't there. So she began to bark at the door as if I didn't know where the front door was. Then she started the relay. Run to the door and bark. Run back into the bedroom to discover that I was still there and bark in amazement. Hadn't I said the word? Then race back to the door where I still wasn't and bark again. Repeat. All the while her tail was wagging so hard she was hitting herself. There are few things in Tan's life that are more exciting than going for a walk and at the moment I couldn't think of one of them.

Fortunately Tan doesn't require me to dress in style on our walks. I threw on a pair of shorts and a T-shirt, laced up my tennis shoes, and worked my way down the hall to the entryway to the front door with a small detour through the den into the kitchen to start the coffee and grab her lead. Tan accepted the delay with squirming good grace once I was moving toward the door. The closer we got to the door the more frenetic Tan became, bouncing up and down, side to side, and back and forth. My usual practice is to say the word "walk" when I'm near the door. It's easier on both of us.

I made her sit, opened the door, gave her release, and then Tan and I were in the great outdoors. I followed Tan down the front steps and along the walkway that skirted the bed of vinca and led to the mailbox at the street. I had deliberately started using the front door ever since I realized that while I never used it, other people thought I did. The basket of cookies I didn't know I'd gotten until the neighbor asked for the basket back convinced me to check outside the front door regularly. It turned out that another neighbor had seen the basket and rescued it—and the cookies. I never did get the cookies.

As I walked, Tan swept the area around me sniffing here and there, sometimes ahead of me, sometimes behind and to either side, but she kept me in the center of her orbit although the length and width of it varied widely. Sometimes I had to call, but she generally remembered to stay close to me.

As I walked along I tried to sort things out. Just how was I going to do what I had promised? When I thought about all the murder mysteries I'd read over the years I realized that I couldn't think of one where the hero had no idea of how to be a detective. Surely there must have been dozens, but none came to mind.

Try as I might, I couldn't come up with a good plan for detecting that didn't start with talking with the police—Jim Ward in particular. Some of the private eyes I read would have started with the cynical newspaper reporter who covered the crime scene for the *News,* but of the two reporters I knew, one covered politics and the other was a music and theater critic. I wasn't even sure that the *News* had a crime reporter or a crime beat—if that was the expression.

With a start I realized I was back in front of the house. Tan was by my side panting heavily. I could feel the sweat soaking my T-shirt. Usually a walk helps me get organized. I can sort through stuff and put things in priority. Usually. Today, I was back where I had started with nothing but a feeling of frustration.

"Come on Tan," I waved the dog toward the front door. "You deserve a biscuit and I need a cup of coffee."

. . .

The Black took offense that I would give Tan a biscuit and not offer him a treat. Tan, on the other hand, had finished her biscuit by that time, so she wondered why the cat was getting a treat while she wasn't. I had dealt with this problem before and I solved it in the usual way. They each got a cat treat at the same time. Evidently Tan wasn't bothered by the fact she was four times as large as the cat and yet got the same size treat. I left well enough alone.

The pets settled, I was considering what to have for my breakfast when the phone rang. The caller ID told me it was Jim Ward. I stared at the phone then at the kitchen clock. OK, it wasn't as early as I thought. Still I was puzzled by the call, I usually didn't hear from him that often.

"Jim," I said as I picked up the phone, "I've been thinking I needed to call you."

I heard the edge in his voice when he answered. "Were you now? How nice. And here I was calling to congratulate you."

I hesitated. There was nothing, absolutely nothing that I could think of off the top of my head that I should be congratulated for. "Congratulate me?" I asked hesitantly, my mind still racing. Nope, I couldn't think of a thing he'd really be congratulating me on. Got to be some kind of joke, but he sounded serious—seriously annoyed too.

"I'd say congratulations were in order, wouldn't you?" Something had happened, something had changed since the last time we'd talked. And whatever that something was Jim wasn't particularly pleased with it.

"Congratulations in order? I'm really not sure that I would—would I?" Have you ever walked on a frozen pond? Wondered if those creaks the ice was making meant nothing at all or if they meant you were about to find yourself swimming in ice water.

"Of course you don't know who I've been talking to, do you? No, let me correct myself. You don't know who's been talking to me and giving me a 'little advice,' a 'word to the wise,' or a 'heads up' about a murder that we'd—I'd already decided was an accident. In other words, advice on how to do my job."

This time I bit my tongue and didn't say a word.

"People like the chief of police, the mayor, and what's-his-name the guy who's head of the university police? Jeff Forte, that's it. Not to mention the sheriff of Shelby County, although why the provost thought to call him, I don't know. I'm waiting to hear from the governor."

"The provost?" I hadn't thought of that. Or, more accurately, I hadn't thought what it meant when he dismissed the concerns I had expressed about how law enforcement officials would feel about my "meddling." Meddling had been my word for it. Aiding the investigation was his. I was getting the idea that Captain Jim Ward had an all-together-different word for it.

"Like I said, congratulations. According to the provost you're the university's lead man on this investigation and we're supposed to work with you." By this time the sarcasm was dripping from his voice. "How does it feel to be the university's Sherlock Holmes? Or is it Philip Marlowe? Sam Spade? You can't think you're Nero Wolfe, you're not fat enough. Though God knows you're conceited enough. Besides who'd be your Archie Goodwin? Maybe you think you're Nick Charles?"

"Jim," I interrupted. "The provost asked me if I'd help. What was I supposed to say?"

"How about telling him to leave it to the trained professionals? How about that for a start? You could have pointed out that Navy Reserve training for Shore Patrol doesn't really compare to twenty years in a homicide squad."

I held the phone a little farther from my ear. Rufus's persuasive manner hadn't carried past the people he'd talked to. Clearly.

"You could have told him that the guy in charge of the investigation had at least two brain cells to rub together and might just be able to decide whether there was a case to investigate! Like he's solved hundreds of real murders! You could have said he's stayed in homicide because he's good at it—not because the Shelbyville Police Department keeps it staffed with idiots! You could have—"

"Actually," I interrupted, "I did mention all of that to him, along with the fact that there must not be any evidence that Albert was murdered or you would be investigating. I pointed out the fact that I'm not a detective. And, I told him I was going to need your help if there was any chance of proving it was murder much less finding out who did it."

There was quiet on the other end of the phone.

I added. "The provost, as you might have heard, is a very persuasive man when he puts his mind to it."

"Yeah, we didn't think it was murder," Jim admitted grudgingly. "Looked like an accident—particularly since there wasn't a note. Was he in love with the guy who died of food poisoning?"

I moved the phone closer to my ear.

"Hell, Jim, I didn't know he was gay, much less who he was in love with."

"There were some pictures in his apartment. Pictures of the deceased with another guy. They looked like a couple if you know what I mean."

"Unless the guy was bald with an ugly mustache, that was probably his partner, Bruce Verne. He's the one who's convinced it had to be murder. Wait, you've been in Albert's apartment?"

"There was a dead body in it, remember? Did I mention that I was head of homicide? Don't you think—maybe—that I'd get a call when a fellow policeman finds a dead body?" He paused for a second. "You do realize how often there's a dead body involved in a homicide investigation, don't you?"

Good. He was starting to crack jokes—jokes at my expense, but jokes. Jim was beginning to calm down.

"Look, Jim, I know that the right way for this to have been handled would have been for the deceased's partner—Albert's partner—to have contacted the police and explained his relationship to Albert and how he believed that Albert didn't kill himself and, in fact, never practiced self-strangulation. In fact, he was terrified of nooses. He didn't have a rope and wouldn't have bought one."

Jim was silent. I continued.

"And maybe you would have taken him seriously and looked into it a little closer. And maybe you wouldn't have. Probably he wouldn't have gotten to talk to you at all and whoever did might or might not pass it on."

"But the guy figured the police didn't really care about the death of a homosexual and if he came forward and told us his story we'd arrest him for 'crimes against nature' or take him out in the woods and beat the crap out of him. Christ, Crawford we're not Neanderthals! This is the twenty-first century! Why didn't you tell this guy to call me!"

"I haven't talked to him. The provost hasn't talked to him either."

"Then who?"

"You know this is a small town."

"Yeah," said Jim. "And?"

"Sometimes, in a small town, things get handled in a way they wouldn't be—"

Jim interrupted, "Everybody knows everybody else and everybody else's business. What I'm hearing is that this guy whose Albert's partner knows somebody in Shelbyville or at the university. Somebody that is somebody. Somebody with influence." Jim snorted. "So we're bending the rules just because somebody knows somebody? You know how I feel about that crap. 'Knowing' somebody shouldn't give you a break where the law is involved. The law has got to be the law no matter who you are or who you know."

"But this time—"

"This time is different?" snarled Captain Jim Ward.

"A little. This time the in-flu-ence is trying to uncover a crime, not cover it up."

There was a pause while Jim thought it through. "I will be damned. So it is. I guess there has to be a first time for everything."

"And I need your help. And not for the first time."

Jim burst out laughing. "I guess you do. You're the one that's got to live up to Rufus George's expectations. You just let me know how I can help."

And so I did. We made arrangements for him to show me Albert's apartment. We chatted about a few other things and then he broke it off.

"From the looks of the phone, I've got people sitting on hold waiting to talk to me. I gotta go. Hey, maybe it's the governor's office? Give me a call and we'll talk."

I hung up the phone, glad that Ward had gotten over his mad. We'd been friends for a long time. Since before Eleanor now that I thought about it. I sat for a moment and remembered how he and Eleanor had gotten along. A little uncertain at first. He said himself that he didn't have many female friends. But then he and Eleanor had got on like a house a fire. They used to laugh and say that having to put up with me made them understand each other.

I tilted my head back and stared up at the ceiling, remembering. Eleanor had just run out to do an errand and I'd stayed at home to do—what? I don't really remember.

I dropped my eyes and stared at my hands for a moment. The Black walked up, cocked his head at me, then jumped up into my lap.

I stroked his head and started talking.

. . .

I remember that I'd begun to get worried that it was taking her so long. You know, the kind of thing you do. I told myself that she'd met somebody at the grocery store she hadn't seen in forever. She'd remembered something else she needed to pick up. The lettuce didn't look fresh so she went somewhere else. She'd had a flat tire—then the front doorbell rang. I flew out of the den to the front door and flung it open to see a man standing at the top of the short flight of steps.

It was Ward—looking like he was trying to figure out what to do next. He'd intercepted the squad car the city sends out in cases like mine. The city fathers don't want voters to get a phone call saying their wives have been run over by some coked-up truck driver who didn't even slow down after he crushed her car. Phone calls are so impersonal. Send the police instead. They loved that duty, I assure you.

Ward stood there with his long face even longer than usual. I looked past him. The front lawn slopes down to the street, not too steep to mow but still a definite slope. His car was parked at an angle in front of the squad car and there were two uniformed police standing by it. They were staring at the bed of vinca surrounding the oak in the middle of the front yard instead of looking at us. Ward had barely beaten them to the house.

If she'd been alive they would have rushed me to the hospital. Hell, he probably would have gone straight to the hospital and let the uniforms bring me. The fact that we were all standing still trying not to look at each other told me all I needed to know. I grabbed the doorjamb to steady myself then let go and stood on my own two feet.

"Was it quick?" My voice sounded strange, maybe it was the roaring in my ears.

"Real quick," croaked Ward. "She prob—" He caught himself. "She never saw the truck. She didn't have time to be scared."

Tan had come with me to the door. She probably had barked at the doorbell. I don't remember. Once she'd recognized Ward she'd sat by my side. I can remember . . . yeah, I can remember stroking her head while my whole world was falling apart. Then she sensed something—I dunno what—maybe how close I was to losing it. And she started barking and growling at Jim, hair on her back all raised up, lips curled back showing her fangs. She looked seriously dangerous. I don't mean "as dangerous as Tan could look." I mean like she was ready to tear some flesh out of her old pal Jim Ward and anybody else she could get to.

. . .

I looked at TB who was staring back at me intently, a little purr going on in the background. "So I started to cope with the loss of Eleanor by keeping my dog from attacking a good friend. Then I had to do something about this and something about that. I've been coping ever since.

"Haven't I told you this story before?" I tapped him on his nose with my forefinger. "I'm sure I have." The Black caught my finger with one paw and gently bit it.

CHAPTER 13
LATER MONDAY

Somebody had called while I was talking to Ward, the message light was blinking. Since I'd been on the phone I couldn't see who had called, I had to listen to the message. It was from Voni. She confirmed that the meeting that I had planned on with Albert and her was still on. Albert wasn't going to be there, obviously, but she felt she would be able to make sure I was headed the right way with the video. She was glad that the provost hadn't taken Albert's death as a reason to delay the memorial service. Sean was being cremated today and she would bring the urn with Sean's ashes to the service. I was glad that I didn't need to call her back. I mean her stoicism at the death of her fiancé could have been explained as how she dealt with grief but her attitude toward Albert's death was more like "so what."

I had scheduled my meeting with Voni and Albert at 1:30. Sean had established Monday afternoon "leadership committee" meetings that always started at three and ran until "the team" had run out of things to talk about. When he was there, the meetings always ran long. I assumed that the meetings lived on, "the evil men do" often does, so our meeting could only run an hour and a half. At that point they would have to leave and I'd have the room to myself.

I started putting all the documents that Albert had given me back into the box. I had kept them pretty well organized so it wasn't hard to do despite The Black's attempts to help. I'm never sure what prompts him to be interested in what I'm doing. It doesn't seem to me that it's any more interesting loading one box than the other, but TB clearly doesn't agree.

Maybe he was a little jealous about the lack of attention he'd gotten Saturday night and Sunday, but that didn't really make sense. Bobby loved cats.

Giving up on that line of thought, I decided I'd back up the work I'd been doing on Sean's memorial service to a USB drive instead of FireWire and take that in to the university. I had an almost empty 500GB drive that I could use. That way I'd have plenty of room to keep the original and make some modifications to a copy.

A room that new ought to be able to handle any kind of connection, but I knew that despite Sean's desire to have a cutting-edge multimedia room, some corners had been cut. Worse than that, there had been a lack of continuity or oversight in deciding what to purchase and install. All-in-all a typical committee-designed room made worse by Sean's management style. Or so it seemed to me.

I'd been the straw boss for the monitoring system he had wanted installed. The one that had captured his dying and my retirement party. That reminded me, I hadn't even glanced at that stuff. As far as the monitoring system, I'd fought any of his suggestions that ignored prior decisions. The man had loved glossy sales brochures and believed everything a salesman said. It was one of the reasons we'd both been happy when I'd decided to take early retirement.

I made sure I'd selected the right files and directories for copying and then made sure one more time. Yep, I'd left out a folder that contained some text files I thought I might use as crawlers under the video. I added that to the queue. "Measure twice, cut once," I mumbled to myself. Not what my old scoutmaster had been talking about originally, but it was universally true. If I'd always made sure I was telling these computers what

I really wanted them to do, I would have saved myself many a wasted hour and heartache.

Having said that, I went back and checked again. This time I didn't find anything I'd forgotten so I said "go" and the read/write lights started blinking. With this equipment the lights were probably just there for the old guys who remembered when they meant something.

The transfer would take a little while so I pulled up some of the unused images and footage to see if I'd overlooked anything. I liked to have too much material to work with instead of too little. I guess everybody does. I was clicking through pictures seeing Sean, Veronica, and Albert in various locations over the course of time. They weren't the only ones in the pictures, of course, just the only people I knew until we got to the recent shots. Sean was in almost all the pictures, even those that were clearly pictures of buildings. Veronica occasionally and Albert almost never. Maybe he was the one taking the pictures? You could see how styles in women's clothes had changed over the last twenty years. Interesting, our Veronica was something of a clotheshorse. I rarely if ever saw her in an outfit at one function that I'd seen her in at another.

Bobby had said that her friends at Mississippi Southwestern University hadn't gotten to know her very well, or Sean either. They'd had a lot of things to say about him, Sean that is, but not so much about Voni or Albert. Not surprising, I suppose. I sat still for a few seconds then shook my head. Actually, it was surprising—astonishing, in fact. Shannons, Mississippi, was quite a bit smaller than Shelbyville. Sean had been there for more than two years. His longest "tour" since he went into administration. There had been those of us who'd hoped he would revert back to his earlier pattern of spending eighteen months at an institution of higher learning before moving on, but it hadn't happened. Either it was the lousy economy or he'd hit his peak, whatever the reason, he'd given no sign of moving on.

What was it Bobby had said her friends had told her about Voni? They had agreed with the Ice Queen description to an extent. And that was good since who wanted to see their boss be all "lovey-dovey" at work. I paused. OK, to see a hated and despised boss be all lovey-dovey at work. I nodded to myself. The hatred part did color one's attitude. I'd best be aware of that.

Voni and Albert had followed Sean to Shannons shortly after he was hired. It had taken him longer to get Albert hired here than it had the other places. Some of Bobby's friends thought that Albert wanted to stay in Shannons. He'd settled into small-town southern living fairly well. Sean had been able to bring Veronica with him as part of the hiring package, or so Rufus had said. Of course Rufus was old school. The Black jumped onto the back of my chair and walked down my chest to sit in my lap. Not the most comfortable approach as far as I was concerned, but TB liked it.

I scratched him on the top of his head and then under his chin and I could feel the beginnings of a purr. Yeah, Rufus would have wanted to hire a married man or woman to be vice provost. What was that old rule of thumb? Graduate assistants should never marry, professors may marry, and deans must marry. Something along those lines, I think. Old school, like I said, but I could see some logic in it. If you just looked at academic salaries it made a world of sense before the advent of two-income families. Hmmm, might be best not to mention that I thought it made some sense to Bobby. Don't think she'd feel it was all that logical.

The Black began to knead on my stomach reminding me that he needed to have his claws clipped. I'd meant to do that before Bobby came over since I thought he'd want to love on her while she was here. He hadn't but that was OK, I made up for it. I put The Black down on the floor and stood up. "A man's got things to do. Can't have a cat hanging around him all day."

The Black looked up at me and I couldn't be sure he wasn't laughing at me.

It didn't matter. I did have things I had to do. The file copying had finished so I unmounted the drive, disconnected the cable and wrapped it around the drive, and started to stick it in the box that Albert had originally given me. It was almost full with all the stuff he'd provided. I thought better of it and stuffed the drive in my toolkit. I called it that, but it was really just a collection of various cables, interfaces, thumb drives, screwdrivers, batteries, and the like, somewhat organized in a laptop case. Oh, and a laptop too. I had had need of all of them at one time or the other over the course of my career at the university. I glanced over it again and was satisfied that I had all I needed for the meeting. All I needed and then some, but I was probably missing something.

. . .

I put the box and the toolkit in the car, walked back into the kitchen and glanced at my cell phone. I had thought to call Stan and see if he was free for lunch, but it didn't look like I'd left myself enough time. I'd have to grab something here and hope to catch up with him after my meeting with Veronica. I had wanted to discuss some of the fades I was using before trying them out in the multimedia room, but it was too late for that now.

Oh well. I headed for the fridge. There was some leftover Conecuh sausage, a couple of different cheeses, olives, and hummus. And there had been a couple of Red Stripes left over, but I was kidding myself there. Beer at lunch was fine if all I had to do in the afternoon was nap. This was not one of those days. I started pulling stuff out of the fridge; Tan and The Black showed some interest in what I was doing. So much so that I nearly tripped over them.

I shooed Tan outside and put some fresh dry food in TB's bowl. I keep his food and a water bowl up on a small side table. Tan believes that food on the floor, even food in the cat's dish, is hers. Living with pets is a series of compromises.

I sat down to eat and look at the rest of the paper. After the *Shelbyville News* had switched to being a morning paper, I'd had to adjust the way I read the paper. That was like twenty years ago, but, still, I'd had to adjust. Anyway, I didn't read it all in one sitting any more. I broke it up, with the serious sections at lunch—if at all.

I'd finished lunch and cleaned up, not that there was that much to clean up. The leftover food went back into the fridge and the dishes into the dishwasher. It was still too early for my appointment, but if I waited much longer I'd have trouble finding a parking place. I remembered the weight of the box and decided to err on the conservative side.

Before I left I made sure that Tan had plenty of water and gave her a rawhide bone to chew on. She still had one I'd given her last week but she'd lost interest in it. I think they get stale or tired. With everything secure on the home front I set out for the university.

I got there with forty minutes to spare and a parking spot on the front row. I started to get out of the car and then thought better of it. Once spotted standing in the parking lot I'd be a magnet for people coming back from lunch who didn't really want to go back to work. I picked up my cell phone and scrolled down to Jim Ward's number. It would probably be a good idea to check in with him. Maybe the paid professional had actually detected something. I got his voice mail and left a message. Maybe he could show me Albert's apartment tomorrow morning.

I saw one of the department's biggest gossips walk to his car, get in, and drive off. I started to congratulate myself on avoiding him when I realized what a lousy detective I was being. Damn, what was I thinking? Maybe somebody had seen something or knew something. And who better to talk to than the man who knew everything about everybody?

I got out of the car and put the box on the hood. I really didn't want to spend more time than absolutely necessary with Veronica. I certainly didn't want to make small talk and I didn't have that much to say about the memorial service. I'd tried to make it a merciful length, not short, you understand, but not as long as it might have been. Let's take pity on the audience while not upsetting the mourners.

I saw Delia walking across the parking lot with Gwen, the parking ticket woman, excuse me, the transportation specialist, and waved at them. "Mr. James," shouted Gwen. "How you been!"

"Hey, Gwen!" I shouted back. Gwen and I could make more noise over nothing than any two people I knew. "I still haven't gotten my retiree parking tag but I've still got my employee tag. Is that OK?" As they approached we kept our volume up.

"Law, you know it ain't. What's wrong with you, Mr. James? Go get that gold tag and you can park anywhere on campus, excepting the handicap spaces." She stopped, put one hand on her hip and began shaking a finger at me. "You get on over to campus police and get yourself that retiree tag. Just because it's free don't mean you didn't pay for it! You worked here long enough. They made you pay to park so you could come to work! What's wrong with you?"

While we had been bellowing at each other Delia had separated from Gwen and eased her way around the edges of the lot until she was standing in the shade, hidden from view from the building. "Thanks, Sister Gwen, I don't think anybody noticed me coming over here while you and Crawford were yelling at each other."

Gwen dropped her voice and spoke to Delia. "Sister, you go about your business quietly while I do mine at the top of my lungs. But we both get things done. We'll get there yet." She glanced over at me. "Get the parking tag, Mr. Crawford. You'll be glad you did." She turned around, walked back into the lot, and shouted. "Bye, now, Mr. Crawford!"

"Bye, Gwen," I yelled back.

Union organizers—that's why they were being so careful. Over the years the university had done everything they could to keep the unions out. They had done everything except give the employees the benefits that a union would demand and get. That explained Delia's concern over who might be listening.

I'd grown up here. I knew students who had been here back in the protest years. They had made fun of the campus police back in the 1960s. The students had thought the rent-a-cops were old, fat, and stupid until the administration called on them to "quell unrest and unlawful assembly." The students might not have been that far off about their intelligence but they'd woefully underestimated their skill with billy clubs and fists. I'm sure union organizers suspected they'd be greeted with the same warmth that antiwar protestors had been. Logically, it didn't make any sense. The cops would have been better off with a union themselves, but let's not let logic get in the way.

"Don't guess I'd get to vote to certify the union, now that I'm retired," I said to Delia.

Her eyes widened momentarily then returned to normal. "So retirement hasn't made you too stupid has it? Or were you told that I'm suspected of trying to 'foment rebellion'?"

"Hell, Delia. You know they never let me into their 'inner circle.' I was always having too much fun making fun of them from the outside." I shrugged my shoulders. "The powers that be might even have suspected me of having 'union sympathies' for that matter."

"Yeah." Delia crossed her arms across her ample chest. "I've been thinking that myself."

I laughed. "Somehow it sounds better coming from you."

"You heard that other one died? Rumor says he hung himself. Either it was an accident or he did it on purpose. Either way he's dead." She cut her eyes toward the computer center. "Seems like it getting to be a bad place to work."

I laughed. "One man died of food poisoning and then another one dies days later. It's not the building's fault."

Delia eyed me disbelievingly. "Two men dead in less than a week and it's nothing but a coincidence? That what you thinking?"

I shrugged my shoulders. I didn't see where there was a connection between tainted potato salad and a silk rope.

"Was that the man that does that awful stuff to his hair. The one who killed himself."

"Yes, that was Albert—Albert Worthy. And he used to dye his hair. How awful is that?"

"Mr. Crawford, he does it to himself!" Delia puffed up in righteous union anger. "You want to do that, you go to a professional. See a cosmetologist or a beautician. Let a professional help you be who you want to be!"

I had forgotten that the community college offered a wide variety of vocational courses. "Ah, of course. What about him other than his being too cheap or too embarrassed to have somebody dye his hair for him?"

"Rumor has it that you are interested in how he died. That things might not be as simple as the police were saying."

I looked at her sharply. "You heard something?"

She shook her head no.

"But you heard that I was going to investigate his death?"

Her face was blank but she nodded her head once.

Talk about a small town.

So I asked Delia to keep her ear out for any information about Albert and his death and then I told her what the man in Shannons, Mississippi, had said.

. . .

I headed for the elevator with my toolkit hanging on my shoulder and the box in my arms. When I got there, the elevator doors opened and it was empty just when I was hoping there'd be somebody to push the buttons. I had my hands full with the box, but after I fumbled around a little I was able to get a finger free and push the button for the third floor. At least I hadn't had to push the button with my nose. Peggy swore she did it all the time what with having to carry Sean's cup of tea and whatever else he'd forgotten and needed her to bring him. She'd drawn the line, such as it was, when he asked her to bring him tea while he was meeting with the dean of the Business College. He was in the dean's office—at the Business College—when he'd called.

I was proud of her for refusing and told her so. Then she'd spoiled it by confessing that she'd felt so bad about saying no that she'd called the dean's administrative assistant and asked her to offer Sean some tea.

Evidently they have a different understanding about what you can ask administrative assistants to do on that side of campus than they do over here. Peggy turned red and refused to tell me what the woman had said to her.

After the door opened I got out and headed down the hall to the new multimedia room. The doors would be locked but at least I could put the box down next to one of the entrances. Sean had combined two good-size studios that had sat side-by-side into one and had left both doorways intact. No point mentioning what he'd done to the people who'd been using those studios. Anyway, having two entrances made the combined area less useful since you had to keep both entrances clear. If he'd "thought outside the box" like he kept telling other people to do, he would have realized that he could have covered up both doors and put a doorway in the office wall that fronted another hallway. It would have given the room more usable space. Still, it wouldn't have compensated for the really big thing that was wrong with the layout—the load-bearing column that couldn't be moved. It eliminated the 360-degree range of vision you had to have when you were trying to create a virtual reality.

Oh well, Sean had had his blind spots and so did his room. But there was some pretty valuable equipment in there now, and the doors locked automatically. And guess who no longer had access to the room? Any of the rooms, much less this one.

I heard a noise and looked down the hall. Veronica and Don Larson were coming out of the elevator wrapped up in their conversation. At least I wouldn't have long to wait. They hadn't looked up to see that I was in the hall. As they got closer I heard Voni say, "You know I don't care about the details. Why are you bothering me with them?"

I faked a little cough into my hand, then once again, louder. Don looked up and seemed surprised to see me standing at the door. I said, "Hope you've got your electronic key. The doors don't seem to like my retiree ID."

"I don't understand why not." Veronica Anson, PhD, appeared to be in something of a snit. Things must not have been going her way today.

Don began to explain. "Because department security policy requires that when an employee changes status—"

"Who do you think wrote that policy?" Voni had stopped short of adding "you moron" but just barely.

Yep, she was in a snit all right. The Ice Queen was with us. She turned on Don.

"You should have left somebody here to wait for Mr. Crawford to let him in. He could have been set up and ready to make his presentation, if you'd just thought. Now you've wasted my time and everybody else's."

She wasn't concerned about anybody else's time. As a rule I try not to second-guess why people do things, but now I needed to start paying attention. Not about Voni, she was just being what she was. However, if you're going to be a detective you have to guess why people do things. Guess and guess right.

Don waved his ID at the door sensor. We both watched as it turned from red to green, careful not to meet each other's eyes. It looked like Don's new boss was going to be just as reasonable as his old one. Provided, that is, that the provost went on with his plan to name Voni acting director to serve in Sean's absence. I don't know that he had much of a choice about whom to name unless he just wanted to make it clear that she needed to get out of town as soon as possible. Anyway, Sean couldn't have been any nastier or more condescending.

"It wouldn't have made any difference." I don't know what prompted me to defend Don other than the fact that he seemed incapable of defending himself. He probably needed his job. "I just got here, so I couldn't have done much. I've got it all on a hard drive. I'll mount it on the local network and we'll be able to share it among the different computers."

I stopped, thought about what I'd said, and realized the flaw in what I had planned on doing. I had no rights on these computers—or on the network.

. . .

If my employee ID had been devalued so that I didn't have access to the rooms, then what were the odds that I could authenticate on the network? Somewhere between zero and none. I'd need a guest account for network access and, odds were, even then I wouldn't have the rights I'd need to actually do anything on the network. Crap. I slapped my forehead and mumbled a few choice words.

"Just realizing that your retiree account's no good anymore, huh?" Stan's cheerful voice boomed down the hall. "Not that your account ever had much clout in that room anyway."

Veronica looked puzzled and, since she was already in a snit, I thought we could be close to an explosion. But what Stan had said made sense to Mister Security. I'm sure it had something to do with policy that Voni had written and promptly forgotten since it would never apply to her anyway but had been left to Don to enforce.

"That's right," said Don. "The contractors we paid to configure the room denied everybody access to the administration accounts on the equipment in the room. Refused to take the job otherwise. Forced us to create a subnet for the room too."

"What! No access!" Voni's voice had risen so sharply that I thought we were about to see lift-off, a temper tantrum of such magnitude that we would all be struck speechless.

"It's all right, Dr. Anson." Stan was quick to pour oil on troubled waters, as always. Today I was glad he did. "It was just while they were working on the room."

Nervously, Don added, "That's right, Dr. Anson. Before we paid them they—how did they put it? Ah, 'handed over the keys' as it were."

"Even better than that," Stan snapped his cell phone out of his holster and started tapping on the screen. "They also created 'guest accounts' that we can let visitors access, so they can make presentations in this room. We'll let Mr. Crawford here use one of those accounts and once he's done," Stan looked up over the edge of his glasses at the three of us and smiled, "we can push a button and undo everything that account has done."

"Sweet," I said, involuntarily.

"Undo what they've done?" Veronica was calming down but it wouldn't take much to set her off again.

"Return all the settings in the room to the defaults established by the consulting engineers after discussions with the client."

I had the feeling that Don had memorized that part of the contract that dealt with security. Maybe he always did. It certainly sounded like it and the dry, legal tone of his voice seemed to calm Dr. Anson down even more.

"What a nice piece of engineering," I exclaimed. "It's an undo button. Damn, can't count the number of times I've wished I had one of those in my life." The looks I got from Voni and Don made me wonder what I'd just stepped in.

"OK, give me the userID and password for a guest account and let's get started. I can get this up and rolling in no time." I looked at Stan. "Even less time if I had some help?"

Stan pushed his glasses back with his middle finger. "Not the first time you've asked for help at the last minute, but after you retired I thought I'd never hear that request again." A big grin spread across his face. "OK, Ford, let's do it."

"What, save my butt one more time?"

"Exactly!"

Ice Queens don't like camaraderie—evidently. Voni broke in. "I'll be back in fifteen minutes. See that you're ready by then," and glided off down the hall radiating contempt.

We mere men stood and watched until she disappeared back into the elevator when we all relaxed to one degree or another.

"I don't suppose I can be of any help, so if you'll excuse me—" Don's offer of help seemed more perfunctory than ever. He walked away, his head down, shoulders slumped. I watched him and wondered if Sean had actually been easier to deal with than the full brunt of the Ice Queen.

"So are we going to put this show together or not?"

I turned back to Stan and raised my right hand to high-five him. "OK, let's rock and roll!"

. . .

The dress rehearsal, I guess you'd have to call it that, had gone well. Dr. Anson, as chief mourner, had a few items she wanted played up and others played down. There were a few facts that she wasn't certain about but without Albert there wasn't any way to check. All-in-all, it had gone well. I'd been able to use Sean's own voice to narrate most of the piece. No surprise there. He'd loved to talk about himself.

I had toyed briefly with the idea of ending the memorial with a hymn. But as I didn't know Sean's views on a hereafter, despite his repetitive comments on how he'd been shaped by his Jesuit teachers, I had abandoned lyrics for something instrumental. I am not an expert on classical music (which is a serious understatement) but the Internet is a wonderful source for filling in gaps in one's knowledge. I decided to finish with the third movement of Chopin's Sonata No. 2 in B-flat Minor, op. 35, popularly known as the "Funeral March." If it was good enough for JFK's funeral, it was more than good enough for Sean. I started recording the music so quietly that I had difficulty detecting when it started, then slowly brought the music up so that you were gradually aware of it. I think even the Ice Queen's eyes were moist.

Stan thought it was one of my best.

And I was still staying afterward to see if there wasn't something I couldn't do a little better—and to play with the equipment.

Albert's apartment was in downtown Shelbyville—a loft apartment over what had been a jewelry store while I was growing up and was now a men's clothing store. I never thought of anybody actually living downtown back in those days when downtown was where you went to shop and malls were unheard of. But people had lived downtown even then.

The malls were built, customers went there, downtown died, and now it was coming back to life—kind of a cycle. Restaurants and bars were leading the rebirth. And with the customers coming downtown to eat and drink, other stores opened up as well. A bakery, wine stores, clothing stores, consignment shops, cigar bars, lawyers' offices, investment firms, insurance—a nice mix of business and leisure. And, periodically, tucked in between store fronts would be a door that opened onto a stairway and the apartments upstairs.

I was standing in front of one such door that I must have passed hundreds of times, never noticing the mailboxes on the doorframe. Albert had cut up one of his business cards so that he could slide his name into his mailbox. The other tenant had just stuck some masking tape over the name plate and written F. Manning on it. F. Manning was in A and Albert was in B.

"Ever been in one of these apartments?"

I hadn't noticed Jim walking up, so the sound of his voice startled me. "Nope. You?"

"You forget who you're talking to, Crawford. I've been in all sorts of buildings all over Shelbyville. This is one of the nicer ones."

Jim pulled a keychain out of his pocket and unlocked the outer door with one of the two keys. "I asked the landlord if he'd meet us here and he just gave me the keys instead—one for the street door, another for the apartment. He's not worried about being able to rent the place once he can clean out all of Albert's stuff. Claims these apartments almost rent themselves. He's lucky it's not a crime scene or we'd have it tied up for weeks."

I ignored Jim's "not a crime scene" comment and followed him up the steep flight of steps to the landing above. There were at least two people I knew of who were convinced that it was a crime scene and I was trying to keep an open mind. Jim opened the B door and we walked in.

The apartment had been extensively remodeled but you could see the signs of how old the building was in its bones—tall tin ceiling, exposed wooden beams, wide boards in the refinished hardwood flooring, exposed brick walls, and massive windows overlooking the street outside. The entrance was at the back of the building. We had walked into the kitchen section of the kitchen/living/dining room that ran from back to the front of the building.

I walked over to the windows and looked down on Tuskaloosa Avenue. I was a little disconcerted to be looking down on a scene that was so familiar to me from the ground. There was a restaurant across the street that I reminded myself would be a nice place to take Bobby. I turned back around and wandered around the room.

. . .

Albert's office had been decorated with university memorabilia—as if he'd been affiliated with the university for years.

Which he hadn't. His apartment, however, was different. This must reflect the real Albert. A spare, clean look to the furniture and how it was arranged. Muted tones of white and teak with occasional splashes of bright colors provided by pictures on the wall or knickknacks. There were a couple of framed photographs of Albert with other people—other men at a quick survey. Except for one that might have been his sister. A woman in camping gear. It was on a small table by the door along with a brass bowl that held Albert's set of color-coded keys and what I took to be his wallet.

The flat screen TV was mounted on the exposed brick wall, stereo equipment beneath it sitting on glass shelves and looking like they were floating in the air. I could see the blinking lights of a wireless router tucked in with the cable box. The equipment looked new—and expensive. "Where's his office?"

Jim looked at me in amusement. "Most detectives would have asked where we found the body."

"Oh, sorry. So where did you find the body?"

Jim shook his head. "Look I'll tell you what we know—how we found things and then I'm headed back to the office. You can stay and look around if you want, I checked with the landlord. When you're through you can come by and take a look at the file."

"That should work. When will you get the results of the autopsy?"

"Autopsy? Who said anything about an autopsy? We know what killed him—the noose was around his neck. Our medical examiner has got the same kind of budget troubles everybody else has. We don't ask for an autopsy unless there's some reason we need one and she doesn't perform one unless it seems suspicious to her—or we ask for it."

"So how's it going getting in touch with Albert's—sister is it?"

"Apparently she's camping somewhere in the back of nowhere in Canada. We decided not to send the Mounties out looking for her. She's supposed to be back in civilization in a day or two.

"Now come here and let me re-create the scene the responding officers found when they entered this apartment."

"Did they have to force the door?"

"Nope, it was unlocked. They knocked and entered. The guy next door let them in the door downstairs. That door locks automatically.

"Anyway, they came in through that door and saw the body hanging from that beam, with that chair on its side on the floor."

"Responding? What were they responding to? They get a call or something?"

"Crawford," Jim growled my name. "Would you shut up and listen? I've got to get back to my office. Like I said, when you're through here you can come by and look at the file. You can even talk to the officers who found him, if you want."

I shut my mouth. It seemed like the smart thing to do.

Jim pointed at one of the beams that crossed over the dining room table. "There's the rope that was used. They cut it to get him down as quickly as possible in case there was any chance of reviving him. There wasn't, but they're trained not to assume." Jim glanced at me. "You want me to go into specifics? About the body, I mean?"

Now that he'd pointed it out, I could see the severed end of the rope hanging from one of the exposed beams. For a moment it all seemed surreal—what was I doing here? I shook my head. "Not unless there was something unusual about it."

"Right. He was wearing pajamas and a dressing gown. The gown was belted closed and the pajama bottoms were on the floor under his body. There was no erection."

I didn't know enough about self-strangulation to know if that was normal or not but I wasn't going to ask Jim—not right now anyway. Jim seemed to be regretting the time this was taking. Besides, since he'd mentioned it, the lack of an erection probably meant something. I just nodded.

"It looked like he'd been using that chair to stand on and accidentally kicked it out of reach. Muscle spasms are part of the process."

I kept silent.

"The noose was made from a silk rope. The rope had been used before and looks used—fibers twisted and frayed."

I perked up at that. "The rope looks used? That would argue that he didn't buy it recently—in Shelbyville. People who knew Albert tell me that he didn't like ropes. Something about finding his cousin dead when he was a child."

Jim snorted. "He didn't buy this rope in Shelbyville. We don't have an adult toy store here. Nearest one is in Birmingham, I think. Of course there's always mail order."

I raised both eyebrows. "Delivered in a plain paper wrapper?"

"Yeah, that kind. It's silk. Didn't I tell you that? Looks like he untied some knots that had been in it for a while."

"If it was *his*. I'm telling you Albert didn't like ropes of any kind. He wasn't in to that kind of stuff."

Jim looked thoughtful. "The person who told you this claims to know him that well?"

"Would you believe if his wife or girlfriend was the one telling you?"

"If there was a wife or girlfriend present, I'd be suspecting them—if I was going to be suspicious. I'd really be suspicious if there was a wife *and* a girlfriend."

"Anything on the table—paper, glasses, anything?"

"Nope. It was all nice and tidy."

I stared at the severed end of the rope and stretched out my hand for it. I couldn't reach it.

"Want me to get it down for you?" Jim reached up, grabbed the rope, and gave it a tug. "Hmmm," he peered up at the beam, "clove hitch I bet."

"What I want to know is how that rope got up there in the first place." I had a theory—OK, just an idea.

"Eh?" Jim glanced at the beam. "He must have put the chair on the table and climbed up that way—piece of cake."

"Easy for you, but not all of us grew to such abnormal heights. Albert was shorter than I am."

Jim picked up a chair, put it on the table top, looked at the smooth polished surface, took off his shoes, stepped onto another chair, then the table, then the chair he had placed on the table. "I'm looking at the top of the beam. He had arms didn't he? He could have tossed the rope over and tied it from here."

I stared up at Jim whose head had disappeared into the darkness above the beam. I was sorely disappointed. "Get down and let me try." A perfectly good theory—Albert hadn't killed himself since he couldn't have tied the rope to the beam—had just been shot down. I was going to have to come up with something else.

Jim reached his hand out toward the rope and stopped. "Huh. That's interesting." I heard him mumble to himself. "Damned interesting—dust of ages." His hand dropped down into his coat pocket and came out with a small, digital camera. "Let me get some pictures."

"What is it?"

"Dust," said Jim. "There's dust everywhere on the beam—except where the rope is—really thick dust."

"So?" I was mourning the demise of my theory so I wasn't paying much attention to him.

"So, unless he was able to use the exact same spot to tie this rope every time he used it, He'd never used this beam before." Jim stepped down onto the table, then the chair, then the floor. He sat down and put his shoes back on.

Finally he looked at me, winked, and said, "I'm thinking that Albert's death is beginning to seem a little bit suspicious. I'm going to get some ladders and some help. If he hasn't been using one of the other beams, we may want to go talk to the medical examiner."

"A used rope," I said.

"And evidence it had never been used before. At least not the way we thought it'd been used. Not here."

. . .

I stayed in the apartment while Jim went in pursuit of extension ladders and portable lights.

The kitchen was small but immaculate. Everything seemed to have a place and be in it. There was a wine glass in the drying rack but even that looked tidy. The fridge contents looked normal. I didn't care for his choice in beer but that didn't mean anything. It looked like a typical bachelor's fridge. Mine would have had some open bottles of wine, but who knows? I can never finish one in a single night without help. Maybe Albert could hold his wine better than I can. I checked the kitchen trash but it was empty. Wonder if the police took the contents? I would ask Jim but I bet the answer was no. This hadn't been a crime scene—except that suicide is a crime. Odd concept—wonder if you can get the death penalty for trying to kill yourself. Suicide was looking unlikely and it looked like we were about to rule out accidental self-strangulation.

A rope that had been used before, not *by* Albert, but *on* Albert. I shivered—somebody had just walked over my grave. I opened up some of the cabinets and found where the wine glasses were stored. Turns out there was room for two more. I gave up on the kitchen and went in pursuit of Albert's office.

I had checked with my cell phone and there were a couple of wireless networks available. Most of them were called something like Linksys, Cisco, or 2WIRE but there was one—the strongest—called banda that caught my interest. I went back into the big room and disconnected the power to the router. Sure enough, banda disappeared. I reconnected the power and watched the lights on the front as the little box went through its automatic restarting procedure. Power goes out all the time and the manufacturers know it, so the box resets itself automatically.

How people come up with names interests me, and Albert hadn't struck me as the most creative of people. Ah, of course— Bruce and Albert. I wondered if he'd been as creative with the password. Banda didn't work, nor did vandw, but wandv did— Worthy and Verne. Last names but he'd reversed the order. Tricky.

I was on the network, as much good as that did me. I needed to connect my laptop to the network to look for storage devices, other computers, printers—whatever he might have attached to the network. My phone—while wonderful—wasn't *that* smart.

While I was wishing, it would be really helpful if he'd hooked up a webcam and had it running that night. Maybe recording to a network drive that wasn't set to auto-erase when it ran out of room. But I was kidding myself. Albert hadn't been that geeky. In spite of that, I hopefully scanned the ceiling but decided that you really couldn't tell from where I stood. Get Ward to check for webcams while he's up there on the ladder, I thought, and made a note on my smartphone to remind me to ask him. I was trying to give up on mental notes since I seemed to remember them after I needed them. If at all.

I gave up on imaginary webcams and headed to what had to be the bedroom. There are times when my veneer of sophistication gets really thin. I don't know what I thought I'd find in a dead man's bedroom, but I did know that I had been avoiding finding out. Bedrooms are so much more personal than any other room—except the bathroom, I guess. And I was going to be searching both of them. As I walked through the doorway I wondered if that squeamishness made me unlike everybody else or just like everybody else. I suspected the latter.

It was a king-size bed and it dominated the room. It had to. The bedroom wasn't that big. Other than that, it looked like an ordinary bedroom—night tables, dressers, an exercise machine in the corner—all neat and tidy, mind you. The bed was made and I liked the look of the bedspread. So far so good. Nobody jumped out of the closet and said boo. Sometimes I can be such a dork.

Albert was beginning to annoy me. Where was his office? The guy took work home. He responded to emails. Where the hell was his computer? A man this tidy still had to have a computer, didn't he?

My offices had always been filled with sprawls of cabling, wires, devices, disks, manuals, cables, and disks. I wondered what a neat one would look like. Finally I noticed what looked like an office chair sitting next to what I had taken to be a dresser. I walked up to it, pulled one handle, then another, and began unfolding a computer hutch or armoire. Hiding it in plain sight. The computer was one of the small iMacs and, thank goodness, judging from the way the screen came up it had been in sleep mode. I was glad to see that it was a Mac. I pulled the chair around. I was ready to start guessing at passwords, but he hadn't enabled that security feature. A thought about fingerprints on a keyboard crossed my mind and I decided a keyboard was a poor source.

I opened up the terminal program and got to the command line. Like most old computer hackers I'm more comfortable poking around that way. I changed over to the documents directory and listed the files by date last modified, most current to least. Interesting. The last file he'd modified was a word processing file named Diary and he'd modified it Friday night. I left the terminal program running while I opened up the word processing program. Sure enough, there it was under "Open Recent." It was at that point that my luck ran out. He had password-protected the document.

I tried the network password, network name, Albert's name, Bruce's name, combinations of both. Nothing worked. I was staring at the screen when Jim returned with a ladder and a trouble light with a long power cord. "It was easier to just borrow stuff from the landlord," he explained. "That way we can leave it here when we're through." He gestured at the computer screen. "Find anything?"

"A file named Diary but it's password protected."

"Well of course it is," laughed Jim. "A diary is supposed to be private."

So I typed in "private" and the document opened right up. Sometimes it's all a matter of luck.

Jim went back to inspecting beams and I tried to make sense out of what Albert had written.

It was a diary of sorts and like a diary, or anything else not written to be shared with anybody else, it was filled with references to one thing or another that meant nothing to me. Even though I wasn't able to make much sense out of it at first, it seemed clear that Albert was not contemplating suicide. He was upset about something—something J didn't approve of—but not suicidal. I wondered if J didn't approve of that either.

Sean's death had shocked him—Sean had had a physical exam recently—for the wedding?—and had told him that he was in excellent health, or xlent hlth, and hadn't been allergic to anything as far as he knew. And who the hell was "she" that he mentioned. Was she business or personal? The writing went from almost understandable to purely cryptic, as if he started out just putting down facts then got emotional. The more he expressed his feelings, the harder it was to decipher.

Maybe I could make more sense out of it if I tried to read more of it—and maybe Bruce would know who these people were. I pulled my keychain out of my pocket, opened up the USB drive that was connected to it, and copied Albert's diary document. I shrugged my shoulders, I had plenty of space on the drive and Albert was dead. Jim probably wouldn't let me take the computer without getting a warrant and there wasn't time to read everything—here.

. . .

Jim walked into the bedroom dusting his hands just as I was disconnecting the drive. "That's it then. All the other beams had an undisturbed layer of dust. I've got pictures of them from all angles so we could prove that point."

I opened my mouth to speak and Jim held up his hand. "And, no, there weren't any webcams sprinkled around that could have recorded Albert's death. I swear I don't know how you come up with such ideas.

"Anyway, I left the rope in place since I didn't bring any evidence bags. Thought I had some in the car but I didn't. I'll slap some crime scene tape across the door as we leave and come back to get the rope."

"Now is there going to be an autopsy?" Jim's remarks about webcams had rankled. It could happen, I thought, but I kept it to myself.

"If I can convince the medical examiner. She's usually pretty good about taking advice. But the decision is up to her or the family. I guess that would be his sister. They are the only ones who can order an autopsy."

"Really?" I shut down the computer and finished putting the hutch back together, hiding the hardware behind a facade. "I thought hospitals or attending physicians could authorize an autopsy and that they were routinely performed on any suspicious death."

"Well you're wrong." Clearly Jim wasn't worried about hurting my feelings. "Nice how that folds up and then just looks like a dresser."

We headed for the door to stairs. "You must have gotten that idea from watching too much TV. Take that guy you used to work for who died of food poisoning the other day. The way I heard it, the intern in the emergency room wanted an autopsy, the resident didn't much care, and his wife refused. The medical examiner didn't think there was anything suspicious about the death. Heck, we didn't either. So that was it. The hospital had no choice but to turn his body over to the funeral home for cremation."

Jim closed the door behind us and locked it with the key the landlord had given him. He checked to make sure it was locked then pulled a roll of yellow tape out of his jacket pocket.

"Wife?" I stepped back as far as I could. The landing was about the size of a postage stamp and I didn't want to fall down the stairs. "The wedding was supposed to be this weekend. You mean Veronica Anson, don't you?"

"That's who I was talking about. Not his wife? Really?" Jim scratched his chin. "Maybe I'm misremembering."

"It doesn't matter. I never understood what was so wrong with her that she'd want to marry him. She must have suffered enough that she might as well have been his wife."

"Still," Jim tugged on the door and took a step back to look at the way the Crime Scene—Do Not Enter tape crisscrossed the door. "The hospital should have known better."

I found a parking space right in front of Will's Sports Bar & Grill—the restaurant where I was supposed to meet Bobby for lunch. Glancing around I didn't see her car. I was a little late so I hoped she was too. Will's was a good place for lunch during the week, as far as I was concerned. As the name implied, it was primarily a sports bar so it was crowded on weekends and at night when the sports nuts in Shelbyville wanted to drink beer, eat burgers or sandwiches, and shout at TV sets. At lunchtime during the week it rarely had much of a crowd. It made it a good place to talk.

The door wasn't one of the omnipresent glass doors that almost every restaurant has. It was solid wood so the sunlight stopped at the door. Maybe that's why I liked the place. Bars should be dark. Anyway, it always took a minute for my eyes to adjust. I spotted Bobby at the hostess's station talking to a tall man with salt-and-pepper hair dressed in a dark suit. She saw me and waved and the man turned to see whom she was waving at. When he turned I could see that he was wearing a Roman collar. It was the priest at the Roman Catholic church near campus. What was his name?

As I walked up to them I was wracking my brain trying to remember and just as I put out my hand the name popped into my head. "Father Fleming, you may not remember me, I'm James Crawford."

He grinned and shook my hand. "Of course I remember you! You helped some of our students with a video they were trying to shoot—if that's the right word. And wait, aren't you preparing a memorial video for one of my parishioners—Sean Thomas?"

I blinked. "That's right. I didn't realize that Dr. Thomas went to your church. I don't know why not, he mentioned the Jesuit education he'd gotten often enough. Sorry about the loss of one of your parishioners." I smiled at Bobby then turned back to the priest. "Care to join us for lunch?"

"Goodness no." He glanced at his watch. "I was on my way out and stopped to speak to Ms. Slater here. I compliment you on your choice of lunch partners, Mr. Crawford. I've got to get back in time for the 12:30 service.

"But it's two parishioners I've lost. Albert Worthy was another member of my flock." He shook his head. "A very troubled and conflicted young man. I wish I could have done more for him. It's all very sad.

"I'm afraid the way we do things in my parish didn't quite meet Dr. Thomas's or Albert's standards. I heard a lot about how things ought to be done as far as Dr. Thomas was concerned. Dr. Thomas made it clear that Albert and he would have preferred the mass in Latin. That's why I was surprised to hear that Dr. Thomas had been cremated. It just proves that you never can tell. I would have sworn that the man I knew would never have approved of it. Why the Vatican didn't lift the prohibition against cremation until 1963. And it wasn't until 1997 that you could hold the funeral mass with the ashes present. The issue being that the remains should be cremated after the funeral mass."

Father Fleming saw the stunned look in my eyes. "Oh, don't think I knew all that off the top of my head." He chuckled and shook his head. "I did a little research after I'd been told what the plans were. That Dr. Thomas had been cremated and his 'cremains' would be buried in his family plot after a service there."

"I hadn't heard about the burial arrangements—I've just been working on the memorial video."

"And that's how I heard you were doing that." He smiled. "I called Veronica to offer my condolences and to see if I could be of any help. She told me about the cremation, that the ashes would be buried in the family plot, and that you were producing the video. Poor child, she must be very upset, the death coming so close to the wedding date as it has."

"Were you going to officiate at their wedding, Father?" Bobby put two and two together faster than I had. I was still stunned that he had known Sean much less the other two of them.

"Yes, indeed. It's a ceremony that I have more experience with than funerals since I've been here at a university parish. The young people come and go so quickly. Still we do have some elderly parishioners. But I do more premarital counseling than dealing with the loss of a loved one. I look forward to weddings."

There was a twinkle in his eyes as he added, "There was a time that I might have suspected a physical reason behind Dr. Thomas's haste to marry and maybe there was. Dr. Thomas was in his sixties and that's late to be starting a family."

"Were they planning on having children?" The thought of Sean Thomas as a father was chilling.

"Mr. Crawford, in the eyes of the church the first reason to marry is to have children, the second being the mutual help of husband and wife. Dr. Thomas was well aware of the church's position but I think it might have come as a surprise to Ms. Anson. It's hard to tell, she is a very composed young lady.

"In any event, I won't be officiating at Dr. Thomas's wedding or his funeral. I'm waiting to see what arrangements Mr.

Worthy's sister will want once the authorities get in touch with her.

"Enough of this talk about funerals. I'm making myself late by gabbing on like this and keeping you from your lunches." He smiled at Bobby and me. "Nice to see you again, Ms. Slater, Mr. Crawford—you make a very attractive couple, if I may say so."

. . .

We watched him go out the door and then turned back to find the hostess standing in front of us. "Two for lunch?" We nodded and followed her to a table.

I held out a chair for Bobby, which she was kind enough to take, and then seated myself. The hostess handed out menus, informed us who our server was going to be, announced that the soup of the day was onion soup and that they were out of chili.

"It's hard to reconcile my opinion of Sean and the thought of him going to church."

Bobby smiled. "Father Fleming appears to think that Sean considered him a disappointment, not being Jesuit. That sounds like 'the man who needed killing' to me. My sympathy is with Veronica."

Our waiter walked up, introduced himself, announced that the soup of the day was chili, that the kitchen was already out of onion soup, and asked for our drink orders. Bobby asked for water with lemon and I splurged and ordered lemonade.

After the waiter left I looked at Bobby, "Since I'm not interested in onion soup or chili, it doesn't really matter, but they usually do a better job here than that."

"I was going to get a turkey wrap. I don't suppose that involves onion soup or chili, do you?"

"No, but I'm certainly not going to order the chili burger. Who knows how that would turn out?"

The waiter returned with our drinks, informed us that the soup of the day was now loaded potato and chili was back on the menu. Bobby ordered a turkey wrap with a fruit cup side and I asked for the French dip with french fries.

I asked her about how work was going at the Press and she told me the latest Philip Douglas story. Another secretary had quit and now the substitute was having to print out all of his emails and calendar entries so he could maintain his management style in spite of the twenty-first century.

I had to agree that—from a distance—her boss sounded almost as bad as Sean.

Then Bobby asked and I told her about Albert and how it was I'd become a private investigator overnight.

"So this Bruce Verne is really from Shelbyville? And from an important family? Which one? I've lived here for years and never heard of the Vernes."

"No," I surveyed the room. Nobody seated close enough to really overhear. "He changed his name—that is if dropping the *r* off the end of your name is changing it. What do you think?"

I watched as Bobby's eyes dilated as she added the r to Verne. "Verner?" she whispered. "A cousin?"

I shook my head. "The old man's eldest son and namesake— Robin Verner is now going by the name Bruce Verne, living and loving in Shannons, Mississippi. Why did he switch from Robin to Bruce—something about Batman and Robin—oh, Bruce Wayne. The family would be very upset if that got out."

"The family have been big donors to the university."

"So they have," I admitted and then changed the subject. "I went by Albert's apartment this morning. It's one of those loft apartments."

"I know. A guy I work with lived across the hall from him."

"Really?" I tried to remember the other name that had been on the mailbox.

"Yes. The police woke him up buzzing the downstairs door-bell at some ungodly hour in the morning on Saturday. He let them in and then went back into his own apartment. I don't think Frank was too thrilled at having the police at his door—or the door next to his door."

"Have you seen the apartment?"

"We're not that kind of friends—just a work relationship."

The waiter showed up with our food and got the orders mixed up. After we traded dishes, we returned to our conversation, albeit on a different topic.

"I found what Albert called his diary."

"Really? Is it helpful?"

"It might be if I could figure out what he's talking about."

"Oh, bad handwriting? Need some help? I'm pretty good at reading scrawl."

"Oh, it's not handwritten. It was a file on his computer. If he'd kept a real diary I wouldn't have found it. Never thought to look for one."

Bobby chuckled and I thought, not for the first time, what a great sound it was. "I should have known. Paper clues are so old-fashioned. There have to be high-tech clues for a high-tech detective."

"Don't know how high-tech it is. He knows what he's talk-ing about so he doesn't write it out. Lot's of abbreviations, vow-els left out, I think there's some Spanish in there too."

"I get it. Kind of like a grocery list?"

I thought of the shopping lists Eleanor used to write out. "Exactly. It made sense to him, maybe it'll make sense to Bruce."

"Are you going to show it to him—to Bruce?"

"I don't know. Right now I plan on going home after lunch and taking a better look at it. I didn't examine it that closely."

"Well, if you'd like some help, let me know." Bobby smiled. "I'm good with words. It's how I make my living."

"Absolutely, I'll keep that in mind." I smiled back at her. "Jim thinks there is enough evidence that he's going to request an autopsy."

Bobby had taken a bite out of her sandwich and there was a speck of mayonnaise at the corner of her mouth. Before I could point it out the tip of her tongue flicked out and got it. "You think the rope was a cover-up? That he died of something else?"

I hadn't really given a lot of thought to what the autopsy might find. It had seemed the logical step once we had thrown out suicide and accidental self-strangulation. "Good question!" I sat staring off into space for a moment. "He wasn't shot or stabbed—no blood. Hypodermic needle? Wait, was he drugged? Could he have been unconscious? The way Bruce tells it, Albert would have to have been totally out of it before somebody could get a noose in the same room with him." I dropped my gaze and stared at my plate but I wasn't seeing the food.

"Albert was a small man but even a small man is hard to manipulate when unconscious or dead." I was thinking out loud like I do with Tan and TB. "The easiest way—and it still wouldn't have been that easy—would be if he'd passed out at the dining room table." I nodded to myself. "Yep. Those glasses in the drainer. Two glasses, two drinks, only one with something in it.

Drop it in the drink—sleight of hand or a distraction. Something fast? No, no need, just tasteless and powerful. Sit and wait for him to drink it—to pass out. Pass out underneath the beam so that all that had to be done was slip the noose over his head and hoist him up. That would take some strength of course, but you could take your time. One tug at a time. Would have been quiet. Nothing to alarm the neighbors." I nodded my head. "That sounds about right.

"Assuming there was just the one murderer, of course. And that doesn't explain who called the police." I came to and realized that Bobby had stopped eating. "Sorry, not great lunch conversation was it? I apologize. That was thoughtless of me."

Bobby gave her head a shake. "No, that's fine. I asked the question." She cocked her head and continued to look at me. "Now I get it. I didn't doubt you, but I really hadn't seen it before."

I raised both eyebrows questioningly.

"What Rufus saw. Why you are going to find out who killed Albert."

. . .

Bobby had gone back to work and I'd gone home. I'd appreciated her vote of confidence—heck, I'd appreciated what Rufus had said—but I didn't understand it. And surely a good detective would be able to understand. I stopped for a moment and entertained the idea that a good detective wouldn't understand what made him a good detective because that's what made him good. I decided that kind of thinking was headache inducing and opted to take a look at Albert's computer files instead. USB drive in hand I headed for my office.

Before I got there, my cell phone made a noise like Morse code. I looked at the screen to see that I had a message from Stan.

"R u home?"

"Just." I messaged back.

My home phone rang and I guessed it was Stan. Sure enough it was Stan on his home phone. "Howdy? What's going on?"

"This is still a land line, right? None of that VOIP stuff?"

I got it. Stan was worried that our conversation might be recorded. When you convert analog speech into binary code it has to be recorded and there's always the possibility that it might not get erased. "Right, no voice over Internet phone for me—strictly copper wire with no computer storage along the way. What's up?"

"The head of Food Services has lost his frigging mind is what's up! He's going to fire all the people who worked on your retirement party!"

"Somebody needs to tell him that Sean really isn't that big a loss."

"Crawford! Those people *need* those jobs! None of them are laughing. They aren't university employees any more, so Human Resources doesn't care about them and they've been too scared to join the union."

"Ouch." Stan was right. Those people at Food Services were probably working two or three jobs and just making ends meet.

"The head has got cases of food poisoning to deal with, one of them fatal. He may be overreacting, but—"

"Have you looked at those disks? The ones of the retirement party? Any chance it wasn't Food Services' fault? All we'd need to do is cast some doubt. You know, somebody double-dipping, sneezing into the food, poisoning it?"

"You've already told Albert and Voni you erased everything. What are you going to do? Pretend that you just found it?"

"I'll cross that bridge when and if we have to." Stan took a deep breath. "You've got the only evidence either way. Have you looked at it?"

"Stan, I haven't looked at any of it. I've been too busy—" At that point I was sorry I'd asked Stan to record it. What had I been thinking? There were multiple cameras each with their own point of view. How many hours would it take to look at all of them? Now I sighed. "Which cameras do you think would have had the best view of the potato salad? Where was it anyway?"

"On the small conference table—at the other end of the one near Sean's office. I'd say cameras seven and five."

"OK, I'll start with them."

. . .

Now I had video files to go through along with the files I'd copied off of Albert's home computer. I had a choice of either staring at potato salad footage for a couple of hours or trying to figure out "grocery lists" to use Bobby's description. At least with the video I might be able to scan it faster than real time. "Might" being the operative word here.

I mentally flipped a coin and Albert's files won. Albert's files had called heads incidentally.

The Black decided that he would help so he jumped on the back of my chair and worked his way down to my lap, making a slight detour to step on my desk and then the keyboard. He settled down and started kneading my armpit. At least he was comfortable. My knees would give out pretty soon and when I moved he'd get up and go sleep on the cat tower. We had our routine.

I opened the computer file I'd looked at in the apartment and started scrolling to the end. Every once in a while he'd date an entry, which helped me know when I was getting close to the last week.

I stared at the screen. "If he'd just finish a damn sentence." I looked down at TB and he yawned, tongue curling into almost a circle. "I guess a complete sentence is too much to ask for when he doesn't even spell out all the words all the time. And what's with the numbers? This is more like those vanity license plates than a grocery list. Like here where he's got c-r-m-8." If I hadn't been talking to the cat I don't know when I would have gotten it. Hearing the sounds did the trick. "Crm eight? Cream eight? Cremate?"

Albert was writing about cremation in his diary? I did a global search and it didn't show up anywhere else in the document—just in this section. I looked at one of the last lines in the document.

J's h8 crm8—not J's way

The jays hate cremate(tion)—not the jay's way. Who had just been talking about cremation? Father Fleming! I sat back in my chair and The Black slid down onto the floor. Rather than leaving, he stayed to groom, licking his paw and then washing his ear.

The Roman Catholic priest, that's right. The Jesuits—something about the Jesuits. Sean had nagged him—my interpretation, not his words—about how the Jesuits would have done things, disparaging his efforts, no doubt. So why would Sean want to be cremated? I tempered that thought, reminding myself that funerals are for the living. More accurately, why would Dr.

Anson want Sean to be cremated? Particularly if it would be against what Sean would have wanted? I gave a mental shrug. Maybe they never discussed funerals. I couldn't really envision Sean imagining a world without him in it but maybe that was my bias. Sometimes when I'm trying to unravel a puzzle, getting that first clue is like the pebble that starts an avalanche. But not this time. I could tell I was being stupid and that just made me angry and stupid. I decided to stare at potato salad for a while.

. . .

I started with camera seven since seven is a lucky number. Actually, I found that disk before I found camera five's—proving that seven was, indeed, luckier. It was a heck of a lot luckier than I was sitting there watching it. I understand that watching paint dry ranks pretty high in the boring ratings—right up there with cutting an apple in two and watching both sides turn brown. Well, trust me on this one, watching a bowl of potato salad can give both of those a run for their money. I admit the occasional person coming between camera and bowl could generate a little tension that paint drying might not have. Did they take some potato salad or didn't they? Could I even tell? Amazingly enough, the longer I watched the better I got at determining the answer. What can I say? I don't think it will ever become an Olympic event.

While I realize I was working with a limited sample size and a small number of observations, still I've developed a working hypothesis that people never serve themselves potato salad from the middle of the bowl. They always start from the edge and work in. With additional funding I might attempt to expand the theory to cover pasta salad.

Mentally and visually numbed by the detecting experience, I decided to make a few phone calls.

First I called Jim Ward. The officers who discovered Albert had been dispatched to his apartment all right, but who had sent them and why wasn't so clear.

Jim Ward was at his desk for a wonder and answered his phone even though caller ID told him it was me.

"Yeah, what?" Caller ID seems to be robbing us of basic civility. I responded in kind.

"So what were the responding officers responding to?"

"Give it up, Crawford. It's internal and it doesn't matter anyway."

I was stunned. "Doesn't matter? What is this—some kind of police cover-up? The police were tipped off to a murder scene and it doesn't matter who tipped them?"

"Damn it, Crawford, pay attention to what you're supposed to be detecting! Do you really think the murderer wanted Albert found so soon? Wouldn't it have been better for the body not to be discovered for a day or two? Hell, if I was the murderer I'd just as soon the body was never found!"

I opened my mouth to deliver a blistering retort about suppressing evidence and then stopped to think. It really was the fact that I didn't know *why* the police had shown up in the early hours of Saturday morning that was bothering me, not that it had any relevance to who killed Albert.

And where did I think I was? Did I think this was New York City? "Bruce Verne was expecting Albert to call and when he didn't, Bruce called a guy he grew up with who's on the force and asked a favor."

"So if you knew that why are you bothering me?"

"Come on, Jim. I didn't know I knew that until—"

"Right, so why don't you go figure out what else you know that you don't know you know—go detect something. Go use your little brain cells!" With that he hung up the phone.

I deduced that Jim's workday had left him stressed. Which led me to infer that if I called him back to ask about Albert's autopsy I would make him even angrier. I suspected that Jim was alluding to a famous fictional detective who used his "little grey cells" instead of "little brain cells" when he told me to figure out what else I knew that I didn't know I knew—or words to that effect.

The fact that Bruce had instigated the discovery of Albert's body wasn't that surprising but the way it had popped into my mind was—or was it? What do I know that I don't realize I know?

That was a *very* interesting question. After a little thought, I retreated upstairs to the kitchen.

CHAPTER 16
TUESDAY EVENING

Once in the kitchen I realized that I didn't know what I was going to have for supper and that Tan and The Black were hungry. I decided to solve the latter while thinking about the former. It didn't take much cooking skill to measure out dry dog food, and the cat's treat was equally as difficult. This was helpful because I was having difficulty deciding what to cook. The problem might have been that I was using too much brain power trying to keep from giving the dog food to the cat and vice versa. Once I was able to turn my full attention to what was for supper I was able to reach the conclusion that I had no idea. I was, however, pretty sure that not eating was not the way to go.

I gave up on trying to figure out what I could defrost and fell back on making an omelet. I checked. Yep, I had eggs, cheese, and ham. I took the eggs out to warm to room temperature—they fluffed better that way. The grated cheese was frozen. I took a chunk out of the resealable bag and resealed it. I'd need to chop the ham but I could do that while the omelet pan was heating. What more did I need? Maybe some scallions and peppers? I went back into the fridge and found a few limp scallions. Oh well, Wednesday was senior citizen discount day at the grocery store. You don't have to prove you're old. All you have to do is look old to the cashiers who more and more look like they're too young to be working.

Tomorrow didn't look like it would be that busy. There was Sean's memorial service, but that wasn't until the afternoon. I should have plenty of time to go grocery shopping in the morning. I went over to the back door and got my phone out of the bowl where I'd left it with my keys and wallet so I could compare the grocery list on my phone with the contents of the fridge and added a few items. I'd given up on paper lists after one too many visits to the grocery while leaving the list at home. This, of course, didn't solve the issue of leaving the cell phone at home, but, so far, that happened much less frequently.

Tan had gone out and come back in. I'd cleaned the kitty litter earlier. Having settled the important issues of day-to-day life, I turned back to wondering what I knew that I didn't know I knew.

The phone rang. I glanced at the caller ID and wondered what Jim Ward had to say. It hadn't been that long since we'd talked.

I picked up the phone and said, "This is Crawford." Funny, that was the way I used to answer the phone at work. Something else that just popped out. Jim started talking without a word of greeting.

"Albert was drugged to the gills—no way he could have resisted the killer. Examiner says he thinks it must have been dissolved in a drink."

"There was a wine glass in the dish rack in the kitchen. Just one but there was space for two in the cabinet. No extra space anywhere else in the cabinets. No wine in the fridge, but the trash can had been emptied. Wait, there was no liner in the trashcan. Who doesn't use a liner for kitchen trash? Nobody with a trashcan that clean—and a box of liners in the cabinet." I paused for a second.

"So the killer took the bottle and glass with him when he left—probably in the trashcan liner. That way he'd get the cork and foil too. Smart. Should have taken the time to replace the liner—been smarter.

"When does trash get picked up downtown?" I was trying to figure out where the apartment's outside trash bin had to be.

"Monday morning." Jim broke his silence, his voice little more than a whisper.

"Rats. There went that evidence. If the killer had thought to put it there. Walking around downtown with a bag of trash might be conspicuous. Might have been hard to tie it back to Albert's though. So now we know Albert knew the killer. Knew him well enough to share a drink with him. Knew well enough to be in pajamas and a dressing gown. But the bed was still made, so his visitor didn't get him out of bed. An unexpected visitor, then."

"Seems likely," said Jim drily.

"Why take the glass? I can understand the wine bottle. Police might have been able to trace it. So take the bottle. Leave one glass in the drying rack in case we decide it was suicide or an accident.

"Ah, take the glass that Albert drank from. Killer not sure if washing the glass would get rid of all the drug residue—safer to take it—quicker to take it." I was nodding my head as things fit together. "That's why the door to the apartment was unlocked. The killer had to leave Albert's keys in the apartment. That's why the police could just open the door."

"The door?"

"Yeah, you remember. You had to use a key to lock it when we left. It was the door to the street that locked behind us automatically. Besides, Albert believed if there was a lock it needed to be used." Who had told me that? "If he wasn't in his office, it was locked." I remembered how he'd locked the file cabinet and hesitated at the doorway before he left me in his office to go and get the printout. He must have wanted to lock the door out of habit.

"Where was his phone? He didn't have a landline—only his cell phone. Did the police find his phone? Do you have it? No, you wouldn't have taken it. It wasn't murder. It wasn't with the computer and it wasn't with his keys and wallet. Must have taken that too. Need to check his phone records—messages—how did the murderer get into Albert's apartment? Call from the street? Yeah, killer called from the street, asked to come up, Albert not asleep but comfortable enough to let person in while wearing pajamas. Had to take the cell phone so we couldn't tell he'd gotten a phone call and who had called."

I ran out of gas. "What about fingerprints?"

"What about them?" Jim sounded bemused.

"Looks to me that's the next step. See if the killer left any fingerprints. At least we might be able to see who else has visited Albert's apartment." I consulted my memory of Albert's apartment. "Not going to work is it? He kept it too clean, didn't he? Can you get his phone records?"

There was a little silence and then Jim spoke. "All that from the fact that he'd been drugged? Would you have been able to tell me who the murderer was if I told you which drug the examiner had found in the blood system?"

"Huh?" I gave it some consideration. "I don't think so. How would that have helped?"

Jim was chuckling. "How about the killer's sex? You figure it was a man?"

I shook my head. "Nope. Either sex at this point. Strength not an issue with the rope and beam right there. Why? Did I miss something?"

"As far as I can tell you haven't missed a damned thing. Not one damn thing. And all of that just 'popped' into your head? Right after I said he'd been drugged?"

I was getting confused. "Well, sure—I mean—it all seemed to fit together. It just clicked."

"I've known you for how many years now? Never saw it coming. Sherlock Holmes Crawford. But Rufus had it pegged, didn't he? Remind me never to mess with Rufus George when it comes to judging people."

Jim had hung up. I was standing listening to the dial tone while I stared at the phone. I put the receiver down and glanced over at The Black. He was sitting straight up with his tail curled around his feet—the very end of the tail was flipping back and forth like a metronome. He, at least, didn't seem to think I was doing anything unusual.

It was time for my supper but there was one thing I had to do first.

. . .

One by one, I cracked three eggs into a small bowl then poured them into a larger bowl. It was safer that way, in case one of the eggs was spoiled. It also made it easier to spot egg shells. I added a tablespoon of water and a couple of dashes of hot sauce then began to whisk the mixture. After I'd gotten it all to the same consistency, I put the bowl down and got the omelet pan out from under the stove. I swiped the surface of the pan with a paper towel to make sure it was clean and put it on a burner. Next I pulled out the kitchen fork and spatula I use to make omelets. I use them when I cook other things too, it's only the pan that's reserved for omelets. A quick glance in the fridge showed me I had a chilled chardonnay. This wine had been aged in oak, so it would have that oaken flavor. Some winemakers age their chardonnays in stainless steel vats, others in the more traditional oak casks. I like them both. I glanced at the clock built into the range and decided to take the wine out now. I'd let it warm a little.

Went back to the eggs and gave them another session of whisking, trying to get air into the mixture. Set that aside, got out the cutting board and the large knife, chopped the ham, and then the scallions. I decided to keep them in separate piles as I might want to sauté the scallions before adding the eggs. I poked the frozen cheese I'd put in a bowl with the tip of the knife, stirring it around to make sure it was thawing.

All the while my mind was spinning.

I had called Rufus and told him that I had done what I said I would do. Albert Worthy had been murdered by person or persons unknown. The police now believed it and there would be an investigation.

He'd congratulated me. Told me that he was proud of me and that he would let Bruce and his family know about the progress I'd made. And then he asked me when I thought the murderer or murderers would be brought to justice—or was it too soon for him to ask that question? He didn't want to micromanage.

I had murmured something about the police investigating and he'd almost pooh-poohed their ability to unravel the mystery, preferring to trust in his creation—James Crawford, solver of mysteries.

I had thought my work was done. I should have, shouldn't I? I'd been concentrating on proving that Albert hadn't killed himself—not on who had killed him—or why he'd been killed. But find out who killed him? I felt my pulse quicken. Maybe I was kidding myself, maybe I had been all along. Some of the detectives I read are driven to bring criminals to justice but others—

others solve mysteries because they enjoy it. And I was enjoying this, wasn't I?

What I was doing was rationalizing. Still, "ever gone a week without a rationalization?"

OK, so far investigating had been fun. Why not see what happens next? I reminded myself of the old joke about the man who'd jumped off the Empire State building and, at about the fiftieth floor had said, "So far, so good." Still, how often does a murder mystery come by in real life? This was my one chance and I might as well enjoy myself.

"OK, TB. First supper and then we start trying to figure out how to find a murderer."

. . .

The Black was in my lap since I was petting him while I talked about murders and motive. He had long since realized that everything I was talking about I'd picked up from murder mysteries and television shows. TB had made some half-hearted moves to get up but always stayed when I remembered to rub his ears. Maybe I should give up on the motive approach and go back to the how. The how in this case being how did Albert get drugged?

The phone rang and caller ID said it was Bobby. I had no reason to think caller ID was lying so I picked it up. "Howdy!" The cat decided that it was time to check the dry food bowl and eased out of my lap.

"I talked to Frank and he says Albert never had any visitors. In fact, Albert was such a loner that Frank's a little dubious about there being a murderer."

I had to chuckle. "Bobby, Jim Ward believes Albert was murdered. I'll take the head of the homicide unit's opinion over any neighbor's. Neighbors are always surprised when the nice, quiet, polite young man in the neighborhood turns out to be a mass murderer. But thanks for calling—Fred? Is that his name?"

"Frank," corrected Bobby. "At first, he was more interested in who 'my gentleman friend' was than answering my questions. But he swears he never saw or heard anybody other than Albert next door. Sorry he couldn't be more helpful."

"Gentleman friend," I thought to myself. And that would make Bobby my "lady friend," I suppose. It made sense but I was kind of disappointed not to be identified as something more along the lines of "my main squeeze." I'd have to work on that.

"Actually, I'm glad to hear that he never had visitors. If the police can find any fingerprints that aren't Albert's it makes it more likely that they belong to Albert's killer."

"I hadn't thought of it that way. Well, Frank confirms that there wasn't a steady stream of people coming and going."

"I suspect the police will be asking him that question in a day or two." I'd tell Jim about what Frank had told Bobby but I was pretty sure the police would want to hear it themselves. "Hey, would you like to come to Sean Thomas's memorial service tomorrow afternoon?"

There was a pause before Bobby replied. "A memorial service?"

"Yeah, wow! I sure know how to show a girl a good time, don't I?" I laughed and shook my head. "Sorry, I wasn't thinking about the venue. It's just a pretty good video, if I do say so myself. We can go for drinks afterward."

"That part sounds like fun—sure I'd love to see some of your work. What time?"

"Four o'clock. Rufus wanted to have it at the end of the workday. He's going to make a few comments and an announcement. We'll roll video, clean up after the guests leave, then split for drinks."

"Sounds good," replied Bobby. "Until tomorrow then."

After we hung up I wondered about what she meant by "until tomorrow." Had I missed a chance at tonight?

. . .

After talking to Bobby, I couldn't settle down for the evening. There was nothing on television—well there never is. I wasn't in the middle of a book. Heck, I couldn't find a book or magazine I wanted to read. I kept picking one up, glancing at a few pages, and putting it down. I was pacing. Kitchen, den, screen porch, den, kitchen, laundry room, downstairs to my office, back upstairs—I was making the circuit.

Finally I stopped in my office and stared at the computer screen. At that point The Black jumped onto the table, glided forward, and rubbed up against the monitor.

"There's nobody else it can be, is there? And only one reason why." The Black stared back at me, rubbing his chin on the monitor frame, green eyes unblinking.

"So how do we prove it?"

The Black had been right. It had been time to go back to the computer. Amazing how much clearer Albert's comments were when you'd made up your mind and were just looking for corroboration. With the right point of view his comments became crystal clear. They so reinforced what I had deduced that I think I had subconsciously deciphered them while wondering what they meant. Poor Albert, good intentions are all well and good, but they're useless in dealing with a murderer.

I'd seen a guy who knew snakes handle a canebrake rattlesnake at a party one time. He used something that looked like it had started its life as a golf club. The shaft was bent and curved where the head of a club would be if it had been a golf club. The guy had been able to move the snake and kind of guide it with the shaft but when it came time to pick the snake up, the first thing he did was immobilize the snake's head by pinning it to the floor. Then he could grip behind the snake's head and pick it up.

That's the way to deal with murderers. Don't get close to them until you're sure they can't hurt you. I asked the guy what they called the tool he used to handle the snake. He'd answered, "A snake-handling stick." Serves me right for asking.

Albert should have used a murderer-handling stick.

. . .

Buoyed with how easy it had been to decipher Albert's notes, I'd gone back to the recordings of my retirement party. I wondered if watching what happened would be as revealing as reading Albert's notes had been.

So far, not so much. I still had too much to really deal with—too many points of view, too much footage. Output from cameras seven and five had been viewed one at a time, then I tried to jump between what I was seeing on five and what was on seven. Not for the first time I wished there had been live cameramen behind those cameras—people to frame shots and follow the scene as it developed. As it was, each camera shot was fixed—catching what it was aimed at and ignoring what was really happening. I froze the images on the screen and sat back staring at my computer monitor. I had so many windows open that I could actually tell how long it took for all of them to stop. I was seriously overloading the capacity of the processor and it had only been six months since I'd upgraded the CPU. I knew how it felt. I was having problems processing things myself.

Idly I wondered what "footage" would be called twenty years from now when the image of handling actual film had disappeared—too much binary code? I shook my head and tried to think of a better way to process all the information I had at my fingertips. Maybe I didn't mean better, but faster. Thinking about how to do it faster gave me an idea. I'd have to wait until tomorrow morning, but it might be just the thing. Tired and satisfied I turned off the room lights and headed to my recliner upstairs.

CHAPTER 18
WEDNESDAY MORNING

More often than not, if cold cereal is all there is for breakfast, I'll go straight to lunch. Cereal is convenient I grant you and a good source of fiber and what not, but there's just something about it that generally turns me off. A sausage biscuit on the other hand—I could eat them almost daily. An egg or two with toast and bacon, a ham and cheese omelet, English muffins, cinnamon buns, peanut butter and jelly sandwiches—all lovely ways to start the day. Provided there was coffee to begin with. I was standing in the kitchen sipping at my first cup of coffee and staring at the fridge. I wasn't standing there with the fridge door open because I knew, pretty well, what was in there. A scrambled egg sandwich, I decided. On whole wheat and I'd add a little cheese to the eggs. I'd forgo the bacon today and make it two sandwiches. It was so early, breakfast would have to last a long time before we got to lunchtime. And maybe I could find somebody to meet me for lunch.

With that decision behind me, I opened the den door and walked out across the screen porch and into the yard. It was so early in the day that the morning was still cool, but it wouldn't last. We still hadn't made the jump into autumn. Tan followed me out, but The Black stayed inside. I preferred to keep him in, but he had a mind of his own about that at times. And reflexes that made a mockery out of mine. At the moment there weren't any squirrels around, so Tan started snuffling through the grass. I sat down at the patio table.

I reflected on how one went about being a detective. I didn't have an established routine, or procedures to follow, or a team to work with. I smiled at the memory of Rufus, so intent as he leaned across the table. "I've seen you, James. Watched you over the years. Don't put yourself down. You can put two and two together and know when it doesn't equal four."

It had seemed a compliment at the time. And then he'd reminded me of some things I'd done over the years that I'd forgotten. Although figuring out who had been stealing money had been easy once I figured out how it was getting stolen. But all of that was nothing compared to this mystery—puzzles within puzzles.

I shook my head, took another sip of coffee and looked around. Tan had found one of her tennis balls and was sitting in front of me with the ball at my feet. I knew what that meant, or what she hoped it meant. I picked the ball up and tossed it down the yard. Tan was on her feet and running before it was in the air.

The prior owners, gods love them, had added the screen porch and fenced in the back yard. That would be the household gods, of course. We couldn't have afforded to do those things when we first bought the house. A friend once told me that buying your first house was instant poverty. I forget who first said it, but the truth of it lives on. The fencing facing the street on either side of the house was wooden, sort of a weave pattern that wasn't as menacing or blank as stockade. It didn't have a "bad" side. The rest of the fence, the sides and back were your basic chain-link except for directly opposite the porch where they had put in about forty feet of the wooden weave pattern. My guess, they really liked the look of wood but couldn't or wouldn't pay to fence the whole yard with it.

I moved my chair over a little to give me a better position for throwing. I don't throw the ball into the beds of azaleas and what not. I try to keep Tan on the grass. I wanted to set up an outline for the day—sort of a schedule of what needed to happen when. First things first, I needed to get in touch with Stan. I glanced at my phone and it was still way too early to call. The only reason I was up this early was because I was too excited to sleep. I'd given up trying.

I reached out, palm upward, and said "Give." Tan dropped the ball in my hand and I snapped my wrist, bouncing the ball off the edge of the patio so it bounced unpredictably and then I went on thinking about the day.

Was there anything else I could do to set things up before arranging to get into the multimedia room?

Tan dropped the ball at my feet and stepped back. She was starting to pant a little. I figure tennis balls dry out her mouth at first, before they get disgustingly damp. I aimed at the bottom of a large oak tree where, if I hit it right, the ball would bounce wildly off the roots and give Tan extra action.

What else did I need to have ready by the time we'd scheduled the memorial? For a moment I was sorry I'd invited Bobby, but I got over it. Besides she said she'd be interested in seeing my work. I needed to see if I could get Jim Ward to come to the memorial as well. Might want to wait until later for that—until I had more to tell him.

I had better take the memorial service footage with me this morning when I left. Might not have time to come back and get it. I smiled to myself. Just yesterday I had thought today was going to be sort of slow. Funny how that works. So I'd take the memorial service along with all the footage of my retirement party. I started drifting off course, wondering again how to coordinate the different points of view from all the cameras when Tan barked and I realized I'd been neglecting my end of the game.

"One more," I said, "and then I've got to fix breakfast." I threw the ball again, watched Tan fly down the yard, and forced myself to think about the memorial service.

I stood up. Tan lay down and began to chew on the ball. She knew how the ball game went.

I glanced at my watch to see if it was still too early to call Stan and realized that my stomach was growling. That's what happens when you tell yourself what you're going to eat and then don't eat right away. I went in and started cooking to appease my stomach.

I put my empty breakfast plate down on the floor and let Tan lick what little there was left. That habit, feeding the animals, was one of the reasons I used my dishwasher so religiously. I didn't care if the animals helped clean up, but I didn't really want to depend on my dishwashing skills to make things sanitary.

Despite the fact that I hadn't left much, Tan was earnestly licking the plate. She took her duties seriously. I'd given in to the bacon. The precooked variety just made it so easy to add to dishes. And it had made the egg sandwiches that much better.

I topped off my coffee and then popped the cup in the microwave to heat it up. Took a sip. Just right. I picked up the phone and called Stan.

. . .

I had convinced myself at least a hundred times that my plan was weak, silly, and stupid. It was doomed to failure and I was a fool to have come up with it. And I'd convinced myself otherwise a hundred and one times. Along the way I'd adjusted the plan—tightened it up—and added some things I'd thought of while arguing with myself.

Everything I needed was in the car, I had loaded it hours before—another drawback of getting things done early—but, I assured myself, if I'd waited until the last minute my equipment would have failed, my Internet connection would have gone down, or the power would have gone out. I went back into my office and made sure that everything that shouldn't be there wasn't—it made sense to me at the time. If it wasn't in my office it had to be in the car. Satisfied, I headed to the door that led to the carport, only to find The Black at the door. I squatted down to pet him and I could hear him purring. "Thanks," I said and rubbed his ears.

I stood up, reached for the keys, wallet, phone, and glanced down at the to-do list I'd made for myself. Everything I could do here was crossed off. I picked up the list, crumpled it up in my fist, and dropped it into the trashcan. *"Alea iacta est,"* I murmured to myself—one of the benefits of taking high school Latin from a most superior teacher. I got in my car and drove across my personal Rubicon.

. . .

Despite the multimedia room's obvious flaw—it had been Sean's idea—it did have some amazing features. As I worked with it I began to see what a wonderful tool it was—even with the load-bearing column obstructing part of the view. You could work around it if you tried. It had been Sean's idea, his overreaching goal, and the greater he claimed it was going to be the more I doubted it. He'd cut some corners that he shouldn't have and spent way too much money on things he didn't need for what he'd been striving to create. But the flaws just made me realize what a powerful tool he'd been trying to create—or duplicate. Few colleges, even well-endowed ones, had rooms like this and that's why he'd wanted one of his own. It was a fitting memorial for Sean. I was glad Rufus was planning on announcing that the room would be named in Sean's memory this afternoon.

I was throwing feeds on the different screens that made up the virtual wall trying to get the timing right so that—as a viewer—you could see the points of view from multiple cameras in real time. Well, I mentally corrected myself, since we can't see in all directions simultaneously, this was in—virtual time? I was striving for the ability to have the screens all display what had happened in a series of points of time from wildly varying camera angles as if they had all pointed toward the same object. It took a lot of triangulation calculations to get the fields of view to overlap correctly, but the computers didn't mind. This was what simulation was all about. I felt like I'd almost gotten it right. I had an object sitting in the virtual center of the virtual room and each screen displayed what you would have seen if you'd been able to look around 360 degrees at any point in time. What you would have seen if you'd been the object, of course.

The object was a bowl of potato salad.

. . .

I'd told Stan that, like he'd requested, I was investigating the possibility that someone had tampered with the potato salad and that's why I needed the room. Between us, we'd agreed that the better cover story was that I was testing the memorial video before this afternoon's showing. I had hated misleading Stan but it was for the best. He'd get over it.

We'd covered the doors and locked them so nobody walking by could catch a glimpse of what was actually on the screens or walk in and see. Stan had left to do what he was being paid to do and I'd set out to see if this room could really be a diagnostic instrument—a research tool—like Sean had claimed.

Wouldn't it be fitting if the room that he had created—the room that he had alienated so many people building—the room that embodied the reasons he "needed killing"—provided the evidence I needed? I smiled to myself. It would be like one of those mystery novels that Eleanor had read. The ones that end all neat and tidy, not like real life.

This was real life and that wasn't about to happen. As powerful a visualization tool as this room was, it couldn't produce anything that hadn't been captured by a camera in the first place. I went back to changing the timing of camera seven and cursed, not for the first time, the decision to use motion-sensitive cameras in some locations. I'd argued for their use, stupid me. I hadn't realized how hard those images would be to synchronize with the cameras that were always on—provided there was enough light to capture anything. I was working on the period of time from when Food Services had put the potato salad on the table until the point Sean had taken a gulp of tea before starting his speech. I stopped at the swallow scene since I had no desire to watch his death over and over again. What I wanted to see had to have occurred before then. I had gotten the timing on everything pretty close, but I was having trouble keeping them all in sync when I tried to move forward or backward in time.

There, it looked like I'd gotten all the angles and timing figured out—pretty much. There were fuzzy areas of overlap the closer the focus got to the bowl, but most of the images were sharp and clear. I set it up to loop and began to watch what was going on around me, as I looked at things from the perspective of the object I'd selected, the potato salad, waiting to see who was going to come into view with poison—food poisoning poison.

But we're not built to see 360 degrees all at once, even though we've evolved, and being able to see behind you would have been a pretty keen aid to survival. Wonder why we didn't? Must be because we're pack animals. We don't need to see behind ourselves, we just need somebody watching for us. Somebody we can trust, of course. Maybe that's the trick to survival, learning whom to trust. That's what ultimately killed Albert. He trusted somebody and that person drugged him and then killed him.

At first, I just glanced around the displays watching people approach and then veer off to one side or another and their backs reappear as they passed. I was impressed, very impressed—but no closer to finding out who had tampered with the potato salad. Even with all this technology, I still hadn't seen the poisoner—at least I hadn't seen them poison the potato salad. I glanced at the time. This was taking longer than I'd hoped but I had given myself plenty of time—I hoped. I stopped the loop and started over and ran straight through the time period.

Maybe this lack of evidence proves that the problem with the potato salad had been with Food Services? I thought about it for a moment. Impossible. There was no chance of a coincidence. I couldn't be that wrong. I wondered for a moment about the potato salad being tampered with prior to the time Food Services had placed it in camera range—on the table—but there had been too many layers of plastic wrap removed for anything to have been done to the potato salad until it was unwrapped and sprinkled with paprika. The paprika was there to add color not flavor—a light dusting of red powder—a common technique when you're dealing with bland looking dishes like potato salad and almost flavorless dried paprika powder.

I started over and took a good look at the pattern of paprika that covered the surface of the potato salad and made a note of which camera view provided the best picture. I stared at that screen and pushed the fast forward button—started out at four times real time but soon bumped it up to eight but all I was watching was paprika—the paprika pattern.

People started circling the table, blocking my view of the potato salad for a few moments, and then moving on. The paprika pattern would be revealed again, slightly altered as spoonfuls were removed around the edges. As the crowd grew, my glimpses of paprika became shorter and shorter until suddenly the middle vanished. The potato salad didn't disappear, but the paprika had. I froze the image, backed it up to the view before, confirmed that the paprika had been there, rolled the image forward and froze it just as the potato salad reappeared. What had happened? I zoomed the image, losing detail as the picture got bigger. I had used paprika and knew there was no way that someone had scraped it off. Somebody had stirred it—stirred the potato salad, mixing the paprika into the body of the salad—the paprika and something else, something that would make anyone who ate it sick.

Bingo. Food Services was off the hook. Stan would be pleased, as would the workers who wouldn't lose their jobs. I, too, was pleased. It was clear I was on the right track. I carefully looked at the other screens noting what they showed and what they didn't. In particular I made note of the backs of people who had blocked the view while the salad was stirred.

I checked the clock—better and better. There was plenty of time. I started shifting the focus of one camera and then the next.

I tried to get Stan to go to lunch with me, but I was too late, he'd already eaten. It had taken longer than I thought it would with the footage, but now everything was ready. It was probably too late to catch Bobby and I wasn't really ready to talk to her. I wondered if I was too nervous to eat and decided that I was too hungry—I'd better eat something.

I stewed around trying to figure out where to eat and finally just left the building to stand in the parking lot. Indecision rules. It was hot standing on the asphalt so I got into my car, started the engine, and drove to the Happy Buddha.

There was a parking space right outside the entrance and I grabbed it. When I got out of the car, I realized that I was on the other side of lunchtime. The peak had passed and now people were returning to campus trying to find a parking spot. I almost lost it then and there before I realized that I didn't need to be anywhere in particular until just before the memorial service. In fact, all things considered, it was probably better if I stayed away. Yep, I'd better stay away. Less likely to screw things up that way.

I walked into the restaurant with the realization that I had time to kill. Of course, there was a table available immediately, a waiter hovering around for my order as soon as I sat down, and nothing to do except stare at the menu. I'd long since memorized the lunch menu—so I opened up the menu and looked at the appetizers. I wasn't sure exactly how my stomach was going to react.

I settled on a bowl of hot and sour soup and a small order of pot stickers. They seemed to arrive faster than the lunch food usually did. My attempts to waste some time weren't working very well.

The hot and sour soup was good, as usual, and the crispy noodle things seemed fresher. As far as the pot stickers go I suffer from a kind of addiction. I've never met a pot sticker I didn't like. Some people call them Chinese dumplings, but having grown up in the South, they're like no dumplings I ever had. I've often thought I could just make a meal out of appetizers and today was the day.

The waiter brought the check and a fortune cookie. Idly I got the cookie out of the plastic bag they seal them in without harming it too much. I snapped the cookie in two letting the crumbs fall into my empty soup bowl and unfolded the strip of paper that had been inside. "A wise man heeds his cat." That would have set Stan off. It always irked him when the saying in the cookie wasn't a fortune at all. The Black, on the other hand, would have wondered why it even needed to be said.

I put a tip on the table and walked over to where the cashier was standing. I handed her the check and a twenty and she handed me my change. So much for a leisurely lunch. I had forgotten that the owners of the Happy Buddha don't believe in excessive air conditioning. The restaurant was a little too warm for dawdling. I headed for the ice cream shop across the street.

. . .

After two scoops of some kind of ice cream, brownie, caramel, pecan, coconut, and fudge concoction, I had a sugar buzz going while wondering what else I could do. What was bound to take an agonizingly long time? Then it came to me. I'd been avoiding turning in my employee parking pass for a retiree pass. With a

satisfied grin I headed for my car. I'd park as near as I could to
Parking Services and take my hang tag with me. I might even
end up with a parking ticket to chew up even more time.

I was back at the car with the free retiree parking pass and a
partial refund of what I'd paid for a staff pass in under five
minutes. Even if a transportation specialist had spotted my car I
don't think there had been enough time to actually ticket it. So
much for that plan.

Thwarted at finding any time wasters, I got in my car and
headed for the Alexander Hall Annex, home of the Department
of Technology. The way my luck was running I figured I'd have
my choice of parking spaces next to the entrance. I settled for the
one next to Stan's car. It was in the shade.

I got out and started across the parking lot when Delia
stepped out.

"I checked it out, Mr. Crawford—the dogs that died?"

"Arsenic?" I don't know why I asked. It had to be. Nothing
else made sense.

She nodded. "That's what the vet said."

I thanked her and walked into the computer center. I had one
more question I had to ask. I knew what the answer was going to
be but I had to ask anyway.

I went to ask Peggy what she knew about potato salad and
Sean Thomas.

· · ·

Stan and some of the student employees had rearranged the seating so the room could hold the twenty-five to thirty people we
expected to come. Since Sean had helped pick out the chairs for
the room it wasn't as simple as it might have been. Who knew

you could spend so much money on chairs? If the chairs already in the room hadn't been bolted to the floor, it wouldn't have been such a big deal to add some folding chairs. Who designs a state-of-the-art-media room and puts in chairs you can't move? I smiled to myself. A man who couldn't resist salesmen and glossy brochures—and that had been Sean.

I admitted the chairs, with their finger-tip three-dimensional seating adjustments, built-in high-fidelity speakers, wireless response pads for audience participation, and advanced lumbar support, were quite the thing. The only problem was that they had to be plugged in to a power source and connected to the network—hence bolting them to the floor. (They were also a little top-heavy with the simulated surround-sound speakers at ear level and tended to fall over if not bolted down.)

The chairs had been arranged in a semicircle, several rows deep; in the center was a podium and beside it a small table. The table was covered with a white tablecloth and the urn with Sean's ashes sat in the middle—the only item on the table. Everybody should have a pretty good view of the virtual wall and the different screens I'd used in the video.

"Nice job," I nodded at Stan and his students. "I see Voni brought the urn."

"Right. Wouldn't have thought Sean would have fit in an urn that size. It's heavy though."

I tried not to show how relieved I was that the urn was there. It was one of the things that had been out of my control.

People had started to trickle in, not wanting to be too early nor too late. The limited seating had made things a little tricky at first but once Voni made it clear to the rank and file in the department that this service was for the important people, not them, things had sorted themselves out. She'd promised to have the service streamed live so that staff could sit at their desks and follow along. She also had it piped into a small auditorium for those who didn't have computer access. I won't mention how good it made the staff feel to be told they weren't important enough to attend in person. The president of the university wouldn't be here—off fundraising—he spent his life fundraising, but most of the other bigwigs would be—after all the provost had done the inviting.

Stan and I stepped out of the room into the hallway and watched as the leaders of the university exited the elevator, walked down the hall, and entered the room. Sean Thomas might not have been their favorite person, but the dead deserved respect. The elevator opened again and out stepped Dean Wilson, the dean of Arts and Sciences with his assistant dean of technology; behind them came Bobby and Jim Ward.

Stan looked over at me and whispered. "I can sort of understand asking Bobby to this thing, but the head of homicide?"

"We're all going out for drinks afterward. You're invited, too." I stepped forward to greet them both and show them where I wanted them to sit.

Just as I had them positioned, Provost George and his assistant, Victoria, appeared in the doorway. I got a nod from Rufus before Voni glided over in her most regal manner to accept his condolences while ignoring Victoria's. I'd have warned her that you ignored Victoria at your peril, but it was way too late for that.

The provost's arrival precipitated the appearance of the rest of the invited guests and when Rufus and Voni headed to the podium the audience wisely took that as a sign that the memorial service was about to start and scrambled to find their seats. Rufus kindly saved Voni from the faux pas of trying to introduce the provost to a group who knew who Rufus was but were murmuring among themselves as to who she was.

Without preamble Rufus introduced Voni as Dr. Anson to the group, explained that she was the deceased's fiancée, and thanked her for continuing to perform her duties during this unsettled period despite her personal grief. Then he announced that she was going to be the interim director of technology, assuming both Sean's and Albert's duties. There was a smattering of applause at her self-sacrifice and promotion. After it died down, Rufus began to talk about Sean and the promise and potential he had brought with him when he came to the university. As the accomplished politician he was, he couched his remarks in positive, glowing, respectful terms that were all, when you got right down to it, vague and meaningless. He announced that in recognition of how this room had been a part of Sean's vision, it would be named the Dr. Sean Thomas Multimedia Room.

After the applause that greeted that announcement died down, he wrapped up his remarks with a seamless introduction to the short multimedia "event" that had been prepared to encapsulate Sean's successes and then yielded the floor to me. I noted the spot where Voni was sitting and the self-satisfied smile on her lips, then I lowered the lights and began the show.

I started with one screen, a black-and-white image from Sean's early days, then another screen, a little more recent. Sean had routinely confided to the audience stories of his humble beginnings and how apparent it had been even then that he was destined for greatness. It had been easy to pick out some of those comments and use them along with the photo trail to outline the part of the video I thought of as "Sean, the early years." I let images linger on some screens to reappear again on others while some just slid across the audience's awareness as we moved into

"Sean, the visionary." Like I said, Sean had made a point of making speeches and Albert had made a point of capturing them. It had made the memorial easy to assemble. I relaxed a little and let myself listen to a classic example of his smugness and conceit.

"The foundation of my achievements was laid by the Jesuits who inspired in me, as a young man, a thirst for knowledge and engrained in that boy the principles of leadership. Once set on that path it was up to me to supply the tenacity, dedication, and brilliance that led to my successes first in the classroom, then the laboratory, and now in administration. Successes I accomplished in Florida, Texas, Mississippi, and now will bring to Alabama."

That clip had been taken from his first annual address to the Department of Technology—the one he scheduled during the first week of fall classes. Corralling all of the support technicians in an auditorium during the busiest week of the school year was another success of his that became somebody else's fault.

The final part of the video had been a little more difficult. I had Sean say, "This is a day with so much to be thankful for," froze the action and brought up the sound of Chopin's "Funeral March" that had been playing ever so quietly in the background for the past thirty seconds.

I let that go on for a moment or two, just long enough for everyone to realize that this was almost the end, then I pulled back the view as if the camera for each screen was receding, revealing that the scene was from the day of Sean's death and he was standing in front of his office about to step into the room to begin his speech on my retirement. I had found a sound clip that I thought appropriate to overlay the image—Shakespeare and Richard Burton—what a combination. "I come to bury Caesar, not to praise him."

Then the images rushed forward, faster and faster, of him walking into the room, putting his coffee mug down on the table, speaking to Albert about recording the speech, nodding and waving at a few other people, speaking a few words, and then lifting the cup to his mouth, taking a large swallow, beginning his remarks, and then collapsing. The audience had issued a collective gasp at the sound of Richard Burton's magnificent voice but then had remained silent.

. . .

I had frozen the image of Sean on the floor on one screen, now on the others the view backed up to focus on the people standing around—all in various postures of shock—then one screen zoomed in on Voni's face as she said and the audience heard, "Was it the potato salad? Sean's allergic to potato salad!"

Burton continued, "The evil men do lives after them." Then, on the third screen I had picked Albert out of the crowd and the image zoomed in as his eyes widened, pupils dilating, clearly stunned at what he was hearing.

"Why did you immediately think it was the potato salad, Dr. Anson?" Voni, thank goodness, had chosen one of the seats Stan and I had targeted, so the baby spotlight caught her dead center as my disembodied voice was coming out of the speakers throughout the room.

The room was set up for remote control and I planned on taking every advantage of it.

"Was it because you knew the potato salad had been poisoned? Poisoned enough to make people sick—some sick enough to send them to the hospital? But not so sick that any of them died."

The Ice Queen sat there, eyes flickering in the intense glare of the spotlight. "Sean—Dr. Thomas—died."

I went on. "Because the potato salad was poisoned." On all the video screens the bowl of potato salad appeared and as I was speaking it morphed from a slightly lumpy surface covered with paprika into a slightly smaller lumpy pale surface without a trace of paprika. "Poisoned *after* Food Services had delivered it and decorated it with paprika.

"But there wasn't enough poison in it to kill somebody—I'm sorry—not enough to be *sure* to kill somebody. To be *sure* that you killed somebody you'd want to use something certain—something like arsenic."

The screens switched from the picture of the salad to Sean picking up his coffee cup and drinking from it just before he collapsed. "Arsenic poisoning, as you know, closely resembles food poisoning."

Veronica Anson was holding onto her Ice Queen persona—she looked like she had ice water in her veins. Holding her head high as she sat, she looked around the darkened room wondering where I was.

The images changed again. This time we followed the coffee mug backward in time until Voni was the only one standing near it.

"But what surprised Albert was why you said anything about the potato salad. Sean despised potato salad. He wouldn't have eaten it. In fact Sean hadn't eaten anything. Peggy had fixed him a plate but he hadn't touched it.

"There was no potato salad on that plate. Peggy knew Dr. Thomas didn't care for potato salad. Albert knew it too. But you didn't—his fiancée.

"Odd, I would have thought that would have come up—particularly since Food Services was catering your wedding—and Sean had made sure potato salad wasn't going to be served at his wedding reception."

The Ice Queen stood up and looked around the room. I thought I could detect a little color in her cheeks. She started to open her mouth.

I cut her spotlight off and snapped on the one that lighted the table holding the funeral urn. I paused a second and then stepped into the light. It was as grand an entrance as I've ever made.

"But Albert was a trusting soul, wasn't he? He probably forgot about the potato salad comment you made—or decided it wasn't important.

"What was important—so important that it got him killed—was to keep you from having Sean Thomas cremated."

"I have never been in Albert Worthy's apartment!"

"Was I talking about Albert's murder?" I forced myself to chuckle. "Let's just take one murder at a time, shall we?

"You can claim that you have never have been in Albert's apartment all you want. The only person who really knows if that's true is dead, but it doesn't matter. I'm talking about Sean's murder, not Albert's. And I have been in Albert's apartment." I changed the image on the screens to the last lines of Albert's journal. Since he'd typed it, it was easy enough to read—another thing to understand. "And I found that he kept a journal. These are the last lines he wrote. Lines he added the night he died."

y did S die?
accident? allergy? ??
S h8d pt sal
V <3 S & S <3 V yes? no?

S 2b crm8d? NO!
S must NOT b crm8d
V not crm8 S!!!
no crm8 until Mon

"It took awhile before I was able to decipher Albert's shorthand. Uppercase letters are people, he used a few emoticons and some words are like vanity license plates, but this is what he meant." I threw up my translation next to the image of Albert's journal entry and read it aloud.

why did Sean die?
was it an accident? an allergic reaction? How?
Sean hated potato salad.
Voni loves Sean and Sean loves Voni. True or False?
Sean is to be cremated. I object.
Sean must not be cremated.
Voni must not cremate Sean.
cremation won't take place until Monday.

"Sean prided himself on his Jesuit education. We heard him mention it just now in the memorial service. And Albert had the same training—the same religious beliefs. Albert knew that Sean wouldn't have wanted to be cremated. That's what he wanted to talk to you about the night you killed him, wasn't it? About not having Sean's remains cremated?

"And what did it matter? Sean was dead—died of food poisoning, didn't he? Nobody was talking murder. Just bury him and be done with it, right?"

I had gradually changed the lighting until Voni, the urn, and I were lighted. She took a step forward.

"But funerals are for the living and you wanted Sean cremated and cremated he was." I smiled. "You had to lie at the hospital and funeral home and tell them that you were Sean's wife. But you got your way." I pointed at the urn.

"You got rid of the body so there couldn't be an autopsy, didn't you? That way it was the perfect murder, right?" I grinned at the Ice Queen and she frowned at me. "You killed Albert to make sure no one questioned why Sean's remains had to be cremated. You tried to set that up so that it looked like an accident or suicide, right? Still it was worth the risk of killing another person to make sure Sean was cremated. Or was it?"

Voni, still holding herself erect and regal, turned to face Rufus. "Provost George, will you put an end to this drivel? I have never been so insulted in my life."

The room was silent.

"Voni, Voni. Your degrees aren't in what's called the 'hard sciences' are they? Oh, I know they're not. If they had been you would know that arsenic is one of the heavy metals." I picked up the urn and, out of the corner of my eye, saw the shadowy figure of Dean Wilson jerk. His degrees were in chemistry. "Like mercury, lead, cadmium, and others—arsenic occurs naturally. And like the other heavy metals, arsenic cannot be degraded or destroyed."

I was gradually bringing up the room lights and could see nods of agreement scattered around the room as people remembered what they had learned years ago. "So here's the joke, Dr. Anson, and the joke's on you. All that trouble you went to in order to cremate Dr. Thomas—the lying and killing? Everything you did in order to destroy the evidence? " I laughed and held up the urn. "The arsenic is still here. Heavy metals aren't destroyed by cremation. Proving once and for all the importance of a liberal arts education." I grinned at her. "You should have taken some real courses in college."

The Ice Queen cracked. Dr. Veronica Anson lost her cold composure with a shriek as she leaped at me screaming as she did, "You bastard, I'll kill you too! I'll kill you like I killed the others." I hit her with the urn and knocked her to the floor.

. . .

It helps to have the head of the homicide unit in the audience when you expose a murderer.

I don't know if Jim always carries handcuffs with him or it was just because he'd been warned. Anyway, I had told him that if I was able to get the Ice Queen to crack, it wasn't going to be pretty. He seemed unruffled when she spit in his face so maybe he'd listened to me. He must have had a unit standing by since the uniformed police had appeared almost immediately.

"The district attorney is going to want to talk to you, you know that, right?"

I nodded. I felt exhausted and couldn't speak right away.

Jim nodded at me, "And we'll be wanting a copy of that video as well, Crawford. Too bad you couldn't catch her doing it on disk."

I shrugged. "I can prove that nobody else could have poisoned Sean, but I didn't think that was exactly what you wanted." Actually, Jim probably didn't care how long and drawn out it was—and how much publicity it generated. Rufus, on the other hand, preferred a confession.

Looking past Jim, I saw Rufus coming my way and suspected I had some explaining to do. Maybe we could do it over a drink. I thought that a drink was called for. Maybe two.

It hadn't taken long to satisfy the provost, particularly when he explained that he didn't want to know how I'd solved it.

"Now, James," he'd held out the palm of his hand toward me, "I don't need to know how a job was done to recognize that it was done well. I'm very proud of how quickly you've brought this to an end. You've done as good a job as I thought you would.

"I'll just assume that you wanted me to go ahead and announce Dr. Anson's appointment as interim director at this meeting in order to lull her into a false sense of security—that she was going to get away with murder." He paused for a second then nodded, "I would have preferred not to embarrass myself that way but it was in a good cause."

I froze as it dawned on me how awkward a spot I'd left him in. He'd announced her appointment in front of the senior staff of the university. I knew he was considering doing so—he had asked my opinion—but I hadn't thought to warn him.

"Fortunately Victoria hadn't released the announcements, so no one outside of this room knows anything about it. And, as Victoria pointed out, I can understand how you'd think knowing she was a murderer would affect how I acted toward her." He reached out and shook my hand.

"Absolutely." I was struck again by how well Victoria did her job. I continued in a voice meant to be overheard, "I think the interim director announcement set the stage perfectly. Thanks again for helping, sir!" Rufus gave me one of his sleepy, satisfied smiles and turned back to Victoria who was standing at the door. I met her eyes and she gave me a small nod—a nod of encouragement, I think, as if I was teachable.

And maybe I was. I think she thought I'd been too much a lone ranger on this and I should have shared my suspicions with Rufus—but it had been my gamble. What if Voni hadn't cracked? That had been my gamble. What if the Ice Queen had kept her cool?

I turned around and saw that Bobby, Stan, and Jim Ward were standing together, eyeing me and, unless I was mistaken, they didn't look like they were going to be satisfied not knowing what the provost hadn't wanted to know.

"So," I said cheerfully. "Help me clean up and then we'll talk about this over drinks at the Polo Grounds?" They responded with simultaneous nods.

"Let me get my minions to help secure the room," said Stan, "and then not only are you going to explain how you pulled this off, but you're buying."

I'm not sure how Stan got away with calling his student workers "minions" but he did and they appeared to love it, and love working for him.

It didn't take long to secure the room and we were off to the Polo Grounds, an old scruffy bar that eked out an existence on the edge of campus. Some people thought the bar was named after the Brooklyn Dodger's home field but that wasn't the case. The original owner, a guy named Ott, had named it after a bar "where he had done his undergraduate work" as he put it. He never got a graduate degree here but did keep his draft deferment, which was what he was trying to do. He told me once that all he'd ever wanted to do was to own a bar. And so he had, until he got religion.

· · ·

It was a quiet group that followed me into the bar. There was something about seeing a person come apart in public that was disturbing even though that person was a confessed murderer. At least that's the way I felt. Maybe the others were quiet since they were with the man who had goaded that person into coming apart.

I waved at the bartender and pointed at a table in the corner. She gestured back her approval and spoke to the waitress who was sitting at the bar. The waitress, who'd had to put up with me before, met us at the table and I ordered a pitcher of the house beer, four mugs, and some peanuts in the shell.

"Paprika," said Bobby announcing it to the group. "Who would have thought that ground-up pepper would be the clue that solved a murder."

I pulled a chair out for her and made a sweeping gesture with my arm as if I was one of the three musketeers. I was beginning to feel the excitement of having pulled it off—of having actually solved the crime and it made my accompanying grin all the wider. "A chair for the lady! Paprika did the trick—paprika and paisley did the trick. Without them I never would have solved the case!"

The waitress looked around the table. "A pitcher of beer, four glasses, and peanuts?" Like I said, the waitress had waited on us before.

Stan glanced at me and then back to the waitress, "Shelly, just ignore him. He's feeling very cocky. Bring him his beer, but I'll have a Cosmopolitan." He looked back at me. "Jerk. Don't get too full of yourself."

Shelly looked over at Bobby, who had gracefully taken the chair I'd held out. "A dirty vodka martini, straight up, Grey Goose, if you've got it and extra olives on the side."

"I'll have a beer and a shot," added Jim Ward in turn. "Since he's paying," he pointed a thumb at me, "make it a Red Stripe and a shot of Black Jack."

Shelly had nodded at each of the orders, not bothering to write anything down and then turned to me, "And for you sir, a pitcher of . . . ?" There was a hint of a smile at the corners of her lips.

"I probably should have tried that at a bar where we're not regulars, huh?"

Shelly allowed herself to smile. "The customer is always right, Crawford. What'll it be? The Macallan straight up with water on the side?"

"No, not today, Shelly. I'm too puffed up with my own cleverness to start with that. Just a mug of whatever real beer is on tap—Newcastle? That'll be fine. And chips, salsa, and some cheese dip, please."

As Shelly headed back to the bar to put in our orders, Bobby commented, "It's sad how that child hasn't learned how to do her laundry. I swear everything she wears has to have shrunk since she bought it. Someone should warn her about washing with hot water."

"Really," said Stan as he watched Shelly undulate back to the bar, "can't say that I've noticed that myself. Jim, what about you?"

"I'm a trained detective. Of course I noticed. I put it down to her wearing her little sister's clothes. Sisters do it all the time." He leaned forward in his seat. "Paprika? What made you think to look at paprika? Hell, what made you think Sean was murdered?"

"I can take credit for him looking at the potato salad." Stan tapped his chest. "Shucks, I can take credit for him having the recordings in the first place. Food Services was going to fire some employees as scapegoats. I wanted Crawford to look and see if there was any evidence of somebody tampering with the food."

Jim looked at Stan then back at me. "You expect me to buy that?"

"It was a whole combination of things that, when they came together, made me realize that it was a murder and who had to have done it. I was trying to figure out how Albert had been drugged when I realized *why* he'd been killed. And if that was *why* he was murdered then Sean had to have been murdered too."

"Run that by me again, Crawford. You had a hunch? I know what it's like to have hunches." Jim rocked back in his chair making it creak dangerously.

"Some of these chairs are older than you are, Ward. Treat them with respect."

"Maybe I would if you'd quit jerking around and tell us what you figured out."

"Let's go back to the fact that nobody thought Albert had been murdered. The police got a call, went to his apartment, found him dead, and called a funeral home to come pick the body up."

"You going to do that thing you did when I told you Albert had been drugged?" Jim glanced at Bobby and Stan. "It was scary. I tell him the preliminary results from Albert's autopsy and he goes all Sherlock Holmes on me. Door's unlocked that shouldn't be, missing wine glasses, missing trash, I forget what else. All of it pouring out of him all at once."

"His keys. The murderer left Albert's keys in the apartment—that's why the door was unlocked when the police got there. And the killer took Albert's phone—it's missing. It all pointed to the fact that somebody had been in the apartment with Albert and that they had left after Albert died."

They all turned and looked at me. "See, what did I tell you?" said Jim.

Shelly walked up with our drinks, chips, and salsa. "The cheese dip will be out soon, just needs to heat up."

"That's fine, Shelly. We can get started with this and by the way, tonight the check's mine."

She nodded at me and walked off toward another table. People were starting to wander in after work.

"So why did she kill him?" Ward took a sip of beer. "And how did you figure it out?"

"Which one? Albert or Sean?" I asked.

"Albert, of course, that's who we were talking about."

"Oh, OK. Albert was upset with Voni's decision to have Sean cremated. The funeral home had to send the body to Birmingham. Shelbyville doesn't have the equipment so they waited until Monday to ship the remains. Albert would have had plenty of time to have stopped it. All he had to do was tell the funeral home that she wasn't Sean's wife. She wasn't authorized to make that decision."

"How do you know he was upset?" Stan reached out and took a couple of chips out of the basket.

"Well, his diary for one thing. It took me a while but I figured out that 'crm8' was short for 'cremate.' Took me a while to figure out that 'S h8d pt sal' meant 'Sean hated potato salad' too. But it was his diary, that and his browser history."

"Browser history?" Jim leaned forward. "I thought you only copied his diary."

I shrugged my shoulders. "And a few other files I thought might prove helpful. Anyway, he'd been visiting a lot of sites all related to Roman Catholicism and burial practices."

"And from this you deduced that Veronica killed Albert?" Jim looked skeptical.

"No, actually that convinced me that she'd killed Sean."

"Huh?"

"Why was it so important whether Sean was cremated or not? He was dead. I didn't see the Ice Queen caring too much unless having Sean cremated made her life safer. And how would it make her life safer? Only if it destroyed the evidence that he'd been killed."

"How did you decide it was arsenic?" Stan brushed some crumbs that were on the table onto the floor. It was that kind of bar. "You'd have looked pretty damn stupid if she'd used strychnine."

"Oh it had to be arsenic to match the food poisoning symptoms. Strychnine convulsions are a whole different thing. Besides arsenic is what she used to poison the dogs."

. . .

"Dogs?" Jim looked at Stan and Bobby. "What about dogs?"

"About two weeks ago a couple of dogs were poisoned near where Voni lives."

"In Waterloo?" Stan looked surprised. "Mighty ritzy neighborhood to go around poisoning dogs."

"If the owner didn't have money there wouldn't have been an autopsy."

"How did you hear about it?" Jim held up his hand as if we were in a classroom. "Don't tell me, let me guess, you've got 'sources,' right?"

"Yeah, I know somebody who knows somebody who cleans the dog owner's house. Used to clean Voni's house as well."

"You don't know she poisoned those dogs." Jim was a stickler for proof.

"Voni used to talk about what she'd like to do to those dogs—in front of the help."

Bobby winked at me over the rim of her glass. "So Voni wanted to get rid of the evidence, but you just explained that cremation didn't destroy the evidence. Everybody knows that."

"Right." I wondered if she was pulling my leg with that "everybody knows" comment. "That bothered me for awhile until I realized she didn't know that arsenic was a heavy metal and that cremation wasn't going to destroy the evidence. As far as she was concerned 'heavy metal' was a type of rock music. Stan reminded me she said as much when we were trying to set up a recycling program for rechargeable batteries. There are some serious heavy metal pollutants in those batteries. After that, I went back to the recordings to see if we'd captured her poisoning the potato salad or Sean's coffee mug.

"The problem with the recordings is that there was too much of it to go through in a reasonable amount of time." Bobby looked puzzled. "We had eight cameras scattered around the area—nine if you count the one that wasn't working—each of them had been on for two to three hours. If I looked at all of them in real time it would have taken what—twenty hours? Maybe more, maybe less."

"More, it always takes longer."

Stan's voice sounded a little strange so I glanced over at him and saw that he was staring up at the ceiling. A ceiling that, in fact, was worth staring at. It had been painted by an aspiring artist with a large unpaid bar bill. It wasn't suited for the Sistine Chapel, but people didn't come to the Polo Grounds to pray. "What approach did you use—the FBI's or the CIA's?"

"Now, Stan," I started.

"The FBI! The CIA!" interrupted Captain Ward. "Crawford, are you in trouble?"

"I didn't steal anything! It's all in the public domain—freeware, not even shareware."

"Right," said Stan, "the only problem being that only government agencies have got, well used to have, the computing power available to run programs like those."

"No, no. You're not thinking about the specific problem. Those people want to peer around corners and see through walls. I just wanted to know what happened to the potato salad and Sean's mug."

Captain Ward interrupted again, "Was this legal, Crawford? Did you get the evidence illegally? If you've—"

"Hush." It wasn't that Bobby shouted or anything, but we all stopped talking and turned to her.

"The two of you stop interrupting." She looked at Jim and Stan and they nodded. Then she turned to me. "And you make it march."

I nodded my head. "All right. Everything is on the up-and-up. Stan was right. I had heard about some software that a guy out at Stanford had developed to prove what somebody had seen—to create a point of view that didn't exist on footage. To create a view that you would have captured if you'd been smart enough to put a camera there in the first place.

"Stanford? I thought he was at—"

Stan had started to speak but Bobby's glare cut him off.

"Anyway," I moved on, "let's start simple. Say you had two cameras both pointing due north that were a hundred yards apart and what you wanted to know was what a man standing right in the middle, fifty yards from each camera and looking north saw. Could you create the image?" I looked around the table and everybody nodded. "Pretty straight forward. You'd lose some close detail, what was at his feet, but you could pretty well determine what he saw at a distance. All right, now add a third camera, one a hundred feet due north of our imaginary man and it's pointing south. Now all you have to do is fill in what was directly in front of you by reversing the image from the camera pointing south. That makes it easier to imagine, right?"

I had to keep myself from saying "get the picture?"

"Now do you have an idea what this guy had come up with?"

"He theorized that if you had a series of feeds from different angles all pointed toward the same general location, that you could create a composite image of what someone standing in the middle of those camera angles could have seen no matter which direction he'd looked—360 degrees of coverage. He even developed a method of creating pseudo peripheral vision for each feed that could create the image that was just out of view—to one side or the other to blend it all together."

Stan was nodding his head and Jim and Bobby were frowning in concentration. "Bear with me, it's much easier to understand when you can see it work. But in order for the software to work you need to have multiple screens, multiple projectors, and, as Stan indicated, some pretty powerful computers. Which describes Sean's multimedia room—along with some rooms the FBI and CIA have had for a couple of years now."

"Oh" said Bobby, sounding surprised, "you weren't able to run the software from home then?"

I shook my head. "I tried, but it was impossible. With the equipment in that room it was possible, it just took a lot of finagling. I'd decided what I wanted to do. I wanted to see what happened from the potato salad's point of view. If anything knew how poison got into it, it had to."

"So could you see Veronica Anson put the poison in the bowl?" The skin between Bobby's eyebrows wrinkled when she concentrated. It looked adorable, trust me.

"No, nothing that clear cut. For one thing there were too many bodies that kept getting in the way—blocking the view. For another the closer you try to focus the view, the more it blurs. The algorithm works best as you move the view out—because one camera dominates the view. The closer I tried to get to what the potato salad could have seen the more complex the calculations had to be and the fuzzier the results. In essence there's a donut hole at the center where you can't see anything." I shrugged my shoulders. "The guy isn't a magician, just a damn good mathematician.

"I could zoom out from the center and as I adjusted the formulas for the different cameras to correct for odd angles and the timing," I glanced around the table, "by timing I just mean that not each frame was taken at the same instant on every camera. Anyway, I kept on doing that trying to make the center come in clearer, but that was as good as I could get—just the blur up close."

Jim Ward took too large a sip of whiskey and coughed. "So what did you see?"

"Well, for the potato salad, it turns out that I gave up and used some software that sampled the image over time—sort of a reverse time-delay—to show that the paprika disappeared. Don't worry, I've the backs of everybody who was between the cameras and the potato salad and one of those backs was Dr. Veronica Anson's back—she was wearing a distinctive paisley print as a matter of fact."

"Circumstantial," grumbled Jim. "Wait. You mentioned paisley earlier."

I grinned at him. "Why don't you find the people who were standing around when she stirred the potato salad? I'm sure that she's too good at sleight of hand for anybody to have noticed her putting something in the potato salad, but stirring it? They'll remember that."

"Sleight of hand?"

"Right. The Ice Queen is quite the amateur magician and she was dressed in paisley, as it turns out." I grinned at Bobby. "Sort of like seeing sails, right?"

"What the hell are you talking about?" Jim complained. "And what about her being dressed in paisley?"

"I'm sorry, I'm getting ahead of myself. Once I'd done as much as I could with the potato salad I turned the cameras on Sean's coffee cup." I shrugged my shoulders. "At first I thought I had the same problem. Too much human traffic between the cameras and the cup, but that wasn't it. No, that certainly wasn't it." I chuckled. "But I got discouraged and time was running short, so I started checking on the memorial service video. I just wanted to make sure that was going to work the way I wanted it to. I was still trying to figure out how to make sure the Ice Queen broke down and confessed.

"I was glancing at the different shots and there was one of Sean and Voni that bothered me—something looked out of place. That's when it hit me. I'd seen her in that dress before."

"Damn it, Crawford," the veins on Ward's neck started to bulge. "You're telling me we got a half-assed confession that probably won't make it to court and the only proof we've got is that it was because you'd seen her wear the dress before!"

"Calm down, Jim," Bobby patted his arm. "I think I'm beginning to see where he's going. By the way," she looked at me, "it's a caftan, not a dress."

"Right, long, flowing kind of thing with big sleeves. Easy to hide things up those sleeves. I'd seen her wearing it in the pictures taken at some party she and Sean had been to while they were in Mississippi—in some of the footage Albert gave me for the memorial. Same dress, same caftan, whatever you call it. I had been through thousands of feet of footage, hundreds of pictures, and one thing you could count on when you were trying to sort them out was what Veronica Anson was wearing. If she was wearing it, it was the same party."

Stan chimed in having done the same sort of thing himself. "Yeah," he said. "You learn to use clues like that when you're trying to sort pictures, gets to be a habit that you're not even aware of."

"She never wore the same outfit twice?" For someone who knew that sisters swapped clothes, Jim Ward was being remarkably slow. It made you wonder if he noticed when his wife wore something new.

Bobby nodded. "Well, not to parties—maybe to work or around the house, but definitely not to parties. She is something of a clotheshorse, you know."

"See!" I said. "See how it's starting to come together? She never wears the same outfit twice to a party, but she does at this one, the party Sean gets killed at, she wears an outfit that she'd worn at Sean's birthday party, right Bobby?"

"So say my friends in Mississippi. They recognized the pictures you put up on the website. They were from Dr. Thomas's sixtieth birthday party."

"Where she had entertained by doing . . ." I'd been over this with her.

"Magic tricks," said Bobby. She looked at Stan and Jim, adding, "Sleight-of-hand kinds of things, you know," she waved her hands in the air, "magic tricks."

"Exactly, and I have it on good authority that she's kept in practice. She performed for some children here in town. According to my sources she wowed them at the Big Sister/Little Sister Halloween party." I glanced around the table. "You know that's one of the president's favorite charities—well, his wife's. Voni was there pulling things out of the air and making things disappear! All in a swirl of long sleeves and quick hands. I guess she didn't think we'd hear about it, or remember."

"OK," agreed Jim, "So she was a practicing magician and we've got locals to call as witnesses. How does that tie in———"

"What do you think I saw from the cup's point of view? Paisley. Everywhere you looked, the first thing you saw was paisley. Understand?"

"What do you mean, all you saw was paisley?" Jim was scratching his head.

"Well, it's a figure of speech, called synecdoche, when you use a part of the whole to represent the whole item. Like if you said you saw 'sails' when what you meant was 'ships.'

"Just tell us what you saw and spare us the flowery language!" snapped Jim.

"What's paisley mean?" demanded Stan.

I glanced at Bobby and saw that her eyes were shiny and that she either had hiccups or was trying to smother laughter.

"Barbarians! It was Voni, dressed in her paisley dress, her magician's caftan, everywhere you looked she was between the cup and everybody else. Don't you get it? I could prove that nobody else could have poisoned the cup because she was between them and it! So how hard was it for her to wave her hands above the table and make some poison 'appear' in Sean's mug with no one noticing? That's what 'sleight of hand' is all about."

"Circumstantial evidence," were the first words Ward uttered. "All you've got there is proof that somebody else didn't do it, no proof that she did it." Ward was nodding his head. "That's why you did that damn fool exposé at the memorial service. With her breaking in front of witnesses like that, the D.A.'s got a case."

I leaned back in my seat, reached for my mug, and realized that I hadn't touched my beer. "Laughter. That's why I called it a joke and laughed at her. I was sure she couldn't stand being laughed at.

"It worked for Perry Mason—every week."

. . .

In the silence, I picked up my beer and took a healthy swallow. From the looks of the chip baskets, my friends had been eating while I was talking. The cheese dip was almost gone and I didn't even remember Shelly bringing it.

Stan and Jim exchanged glances. "Perry Mason?" said Stan and they both shook their heads.

"Don't you remember those old Perry Mason TV shows?" asked Bobby cheerfully. "I've seen them in reruns. It's like Ford says, 'The moral of most Perry Mason shows is to be very careful whom you laugh at—especially somebody holding a gun.'"

"If he's Perry Mason, what does that make you," asked Ward. "Paul Drake or Della Street?"

"Della," said Stan promptly. "I seem to remember that Della was pretty hot."

I glared at him, but he just grinned and shrugged his shoulders.

Bobby ignored the hot comment, or maybe she didn't. "Oh, I didn't do anything to help. He figured it out all on his own."

Ward snorted. "Yeah, like he figured out paisley, caftan, and the magic tricks."

"Don't forget the 'synecdoche' comment," added Stan. "You know he says stuff like that all the time."

"Everybody ready for another drink?" I looked over at the bar and waved at Shelly.

"You're both right, and Ms. Slater is being very modest. She was of enormous assistance. I could not have come as close as I have to figuring out what happened and why without her."

"Wait a minute!" Bobby sat up straight and stared at me. "You know *why* she killed Sean? Not just how?"

"Other than the fact that he needed killing? I believe I do."

"Well," she said, sitting back and nodding her head, "let's hear it."

At that moment Shelly stepped up to the table. "Another round?"

"Sure," I replied. Stan did too, but Bobby was still nursing her drink; Ward agreed to another beer minus the chaser.

"Now remember I was on the search committee that interviewed Dr. Sean Thomas before he was hired by the executive committee. So I know something about his track record before he came here." I looked around the table. "One thing that I thought was clear from the start was that Dr. Thomas brought a management team with him—Dr. Veronica Anson and Albert Worthy, MBA.

"During the interview process, Sean denied that he needed either one of them to manage the Department of Technology. Albert was a friend that he had given a job to who was happy to stay there, but Dr. Anson was more than a friend. They planned on getting married. That went over pretty well with the hiring committee. They weren't keen on hiring three people to do what Marcia Barnes, Dr. Thomas's predecessor, had done all by herself. And the fact that he was unmarried had worried some. There was a little dickering or horse-trading that went on behind closed doors, but the university ended up offering Sean and Voni positions. My guess is that they cut his salary to fund hers— since it was going to end up in the same pot, as it were."

I shrugged my shoulders. "After a while Sean must have realized that what he should have said was that he had to have Albert, and Voni could take care of herself. Sean was a great idea man, he could sell his vision of how things should be, but he couldn't manage his way out of a paper bag. Besides having a violent temper and a tremendously inflated ego, he had little or no aptitude for management. Albert was the man who could make things work—and do it while making Dr. Thomas look good."

"So why didn't he?" Jim cocked his head at me as he fished around in the basket for one of the remaining chips. "The man wasn't stupid was he? Or was he so much in love with Veronica?"

"He needed Voni socially. An attractive woman to escort to university functions. I don't think he was in love with anybody but himself. If anything he might have been more interested in Albert."

Bobby spoke up, "Voni is in love with Voni and nobody else."

We all turned to look at her.

"Crawford asked me to find out what I could about them because I know some people over in Shannons, Mississippi—colleagues and friends. They were happy to tell me what they knew and who else to ask. Turns out Dr. Anson got her undergraduate degree at a woman's college in Columbus, Mississippi. I've got a very good friend who matriculated there and she knew Ronnie, as she called herself then."

"Ronnie?" said Stan. "Oh, short for Veronica. I thought Voni was her nickname."

"It is now. Back then she was going through her butch stage so she used Ronnie. She was pretty convincing I'm told."

I had heard all this before so I got to enjoy the stunned looks on my male friends' faces as they adjusted their perspectives. "The Ice Queen?" murmured Stan questioningly.

"She was experimenting," explained Bobby. "A common enough thing to do in college, especially when people are ambivalent about their sexuality. My friend happens to be a psychiatrist. She was head of women's studies and did some individual counseling while she was there."

Ward frowned seeing a reason evidence might not be admissible, a constant concern of his. "Dr. Anson went to this woman for counseling?"

"Jim Ward!" Bobby was shocked. "There's no way Anne would have told me anything if Veronica had been her patient. No, she tried to help some of Ronnie's ex-partners and that's how she recognized her for what she is. It helped that some of those girls had gone to high school with Veronica and talked about what she was like then. You know, we say it's a small world, but I wonder if we realize just how small it is."

. . .

Bobby sat still for a moment. "Anne's assessment is that Dr. Anson is extremely independent, reserved, and asexual. She hates physical contact from either sex but wants to be seen as desirable by everybody. So she dresses in the height of fashion, has an escort to the best social events, keeps everybody at arm's length, and is scared to death that somebody is going to touch her." Bobby looked around the table. "The thought of actually marrying Sean must have terrified her."

"That's when Rufus, with the best intentions, raised the stakes and forced Sean's hand." I leaned forward and ran my fingertip through one of the water rings my once-frosted beer mug had made on the table. "I told you how Sean had presented Veronica as his bride-to-be to the hiring committee. He told the provost the same tale at their last meeting before he was hired, even though I would think Sean would have known by then that Veronica was never willingly going to pick a date." I thought for a second. "But I may be underestimating the arrogance of the man. Maybe he couldn't conceive of any woman not wanting to marry him.

"After he was hired, Sean went about trying to run things without Albert to smooth things out, follow up, pay attention to details, and manage people. It was a disaster, as I can personally testify. People were signing up for early retirement left and right, but that gave Dr. Thomas the chance to hire replacements. He posted a job as deputy director and waited for Albert to apply. The closing day came and went and Albert Worthy, MBA, wasn't in the pool of applicants.

"Sean couldn't believe it. He had to have Albert. He'd made too many promises about things he couldn't follow through on. People were beginning to notice that programs weren't turning out like he had said they would and some projects never got started at all. Morale at the Department of Technology was so low that it would have had to look up at a snake. In every place he'd been before, by the time he'd been there that long, everyone knew to run plans, requests, ideas, personnel issues through Albert. Sean could go on with his speeches, lectures, visionary plans, and whatever else he did while Albert actually got things done.

"Dr. Sean Thomas had to have Albert Worthy as deputy director and it had to happen soon."

"But Albert was happy where he was," interrupted Bobby. "He didn't want to leave Mississippi."

"Right! He might have been happy for the first time in his adult life. That was something else we learned from your friends." I looked at Jim and Stan. "Why Albert didn't want to leave and why, I suspect, Sean forced him to."

"What?" Bobby looked surprised. "My friends just said that he had 'found himself' and that he came out of the closet!"

"Only to go right back in it when he followed Sean here. When Sean forced him here, I mean." I thought about it for a second. "Yeah, and probably forced him back into the closet as well."

"My friends were surprised that Albert applied for the job. Albert and Bruce had been such a happy couple." Bobby cocked her head at me. "They wondered what had happened. What had caused the breakup."

I held up my hands in surrender. "I honestly don't know what Sean did. I do know that Bruce's real name isn't Bruce and that he is originally from Alabama, not only from Alabama, but also a member of a very distinguished family that is pleased he's changed his name and moved out of state if only to placate their patriarch. It's clear enough that Albert got pressured and moved here while Bruce couldn't. What's not clear is how Sean forced him to."

Stan looked grim. "You told us yourself that Albert was Roman Catholic and Jesuit-trained. The church may have eased it's stance about cremation, but not homosexuals. I can guess that Sean used emotional blackmail on Albert—and I'd bet that Albert had some major guilt issues as well. Maybe he was punishing himself. Was he going to church?"

Bobby nodded. "Father Fleming knew him. Called him a 'very troubled and conflicted young man' when he was talking to us."

I held up my hand to stop her. "Now let's add the final piece to the puzzle—if not the final piece then at least the final straw—good intentions. It's been my experience that whenever I do something from 'good intentions' it is guaranteed to blow up in my face.

"Evidently, Provost Rufus George has had a different set of life experiences. He still tries to do things with the best intentions in the world."

"Oh my," murmured Bobby.

"He had noticed the sudden increase in early retirements in areas that reported to Dr. Thomas. He'd expected some of that since he'd formed his own opinion of Sean Thomas—independent of the hiring committee's. But the complaints from other areas about unmet promises and missed deadlines kept getting louder and more frequent. That's when he called Sean in for a 'little talk.'

"Sean was not a stupid man. He knew that when Provost George had his administrative assistant set up a 'little talk' with someone, it was serious. I'm sure it made him even more nervous when Victoria didn't give him any clue as to what the talk was going to be about. She wouldn't have told him if she'd known, but Rufus wouldn't have told her. He's too much of a southern gentleman to tell her that he wanted to know if Sean was going to 'do right' by Veronica Anson."

I smiled to myself. "You see Rufus was getting ready to fire Dr. Sean Thomas, but before he did that he wanted Sean to live up to his obligations—his personal responsibilities. The university had hired this woman because she was going to be his wife, and Rufus, God bless his soul, thought he'd give Sean one more chance to do that before Rufus fired him."

My three friends sat there staring at me as if I'd grown another head. Finally Bobby began to nod, slowly at first, then faster. "Yes, that actually sounds like something Rufus would do. He probably even hinted that if Sean and Voni married he'd give the newlyweds time to find positions elsewhere—as long as they left."

I smiled at her. "That's what I think happened. Rufus wouldn't come right out and admit that, but he says he gave him a little push.

"So Sean leaves this meeting with the provost and tells the Ice Queen that the jig is up. She has to marry him because otherwise they're both going to get fired. And if they got fired the word would be out and they'd never work in academia again." Stan nodded. "Sean had to have time to find another position. All Voni had to do was to marry him. Because of the football schedule, the wedding had to be this weekend. We've got home games for three straight weekends afterward."

"And that's why she killed him?" Jim sounded a little skeptical.

"Think about it from her point of view. It was all well and good for Sean to say their careers were in danger, but it was Sean who was on the hot seat, not Voni. In fact, if Sean died, Voni would almost certainly have been first in line to replace him." I took the last swallow of my beer. "At first, I think she was going along with it—the marriage that is. Sean was steamrolling her. Then they had their premarital sessions with Father Fleming and that's when things hit the fan."

Stan scratched his ear. "What do you mean? From what I hear Father Fleming is a good guy."

"I'm sure he is. But he's also a Roman Catholic priest doing a rush job of getting a couple ready for marriage. And Sean Thomas was a very conservative Roman Catholic—he wanted Fleming to go back to saying Mass in Latin."

"So?"

"So, as Father Fleming explained to me when I went to consult with him yesterday, 'in the eyes of the church the first reason to marry is to have children.'"

There was silence around the table. I shrugged my shoulders.

"Let's just say that, in the end, she considered murder to be the lesser of two evils."

"But what about killing Albert?" Stan looked confused. "How did she do that?"

"That was pretty straightforward once she'd killed Sean. She had to kill him to cover up the only evidence that would prove she'd poisoned Sean only we'd never have known if she'd just buried the man. Isn't hindsight wonderful?

"Albert called Veronica and told her that Sean hadn't wanted to be cremated and asked her to stop it. He may have left the message on her phone because the next thing he heard from her was that she was outside his apartment and wanted to talk to him. Albert was in his pajamas but agreed to let her in." Looking around the table I saw that I had everybody's attention.

"If Veronica had been a man, he might have changed clothes, but he was comfortable dealing with her while dressed for bed. She brought a bottle of wine with her—couldn't leave that to chance—and suggested they have a drink and discuss what arrangements Sean would prefer—she probably said that she'd been so upset by his death that she hadn't been thinking when she agreed to cremation.

"We know that she excels at sleight-of-hand so it was no challenge to drop something in his drink. At first I wondered if she'd already spiked the wine, but she could depend on her sleight-of-hand skills to put the drug in his wine and having him pull the cork on a new bottle of wine would have allayed his suspicions, if he'd had any.

"Once he passed out at the table, she was able to put a chair on the table, climb up on the table, on the chair, and flip one end of the rope over the beam. She then slipped a noose over his head and, using the leverage the rope and beam provided, hoisted his unconscious body into the air. His weight took care of the rest.

"She went to the kitchen, rinsed out her glass of wine and put it in the wine rack, tossed the other glass and bottle of wine into the trash, and took the liner and contents along with Albert's phone with her as she left the apartment with the door unlocked. The door to the outside opens from the inside. What else?" I thought for a second. "Oh, she pulled his pajama bottoms off and dropped them on the floor under the body. Maybe she just untied the drawstring and they fell off. And tipped over a chair as if he'd kicked it over, setting the scene for either accidental death by self-strangulation or suicide."

I glanced around the table finally settling on Jim. "If you can get the phone records you might be able to put her on trial for Albert's murder too. She's far too smart not to have gotten rid of Albert's phone."

Jim Ward nodded his head in agreement. "Yep, it all hangs together. Good job, Crawford."

He stood up and put his hand out. We shook hands. "Thanks, Jim. Coming from you that means a lot."

Smiling he turned away from the table, walked a few steps, and stopped to pull his cell phone out of his pocket. Typical Jim, he must have had it on vibrate while we were talking. Now he was checking his messages.

Still sitting, Stan looked at me and then at my empty beer mug. "Are we going to celebrate the success of the university's very own private detective with round after round of drinks?" He sounded hopeful. "The Sherlock Holmes of Alabama? Surely we should toast this success and your future successes as you go on to solve murder after murder!" He looked at me and added sadly,

"Or are we going to be old and wise and go home after two drinks?"

"Well, I appreciate your enthusiasm for this new career ahead of me, but the last murder on campus before this one was a duel fought pre–Civil War—and nobody needed a detective to figure out 'who done it.' If I'm depending on solving murders for the university to keep me busy, I'd better get another hobby." I tapped my chest, "Speaking for myself, I'm paying for two celebratory rounds and then going home to feed the dog."

Shelly appeared out of nowhere, as any really good waitress does. "Can I get anybody another drink? Something to eat?"

"No, Shelly, not for me. I'll take the check for what damage we've done so far. See if you can talk the rest of them into staying. Heck, they haven't spent any money yet."

I looked over at Bobby who had finally finished her martini. "After I feed Tan and The Black, I'll fix myself something to eat. I could cook for two . . . ?" I raised my eyebrows in what I hoped was a hopeful instead of lecherous look.

Bobby smiled and shook her head no. "Sorry, but I'm headed back to the Press. I've got a project that's due soon and it's easier to work when 'the Beast' has left for the day."

Stan sat back. "Sorry, Shelly, but if it's up to me to keep the party going, you'd better get the check for Mr. Holmes."

I held my hand up to forestall any confusion. When a conversation she really wasn't listening to in the first place went too far afield, Shelly got lost. "Not Mr. Holmes, Shelly, just James F. Crawford like it says on the credit card." I held up my piece of plastic and Shelly took it with her as she headed for the bar.

Captain Jim Ward had begun to pace back and forth as he listened to his phone messages and returned some calls. Now he turned and came back to the table.

Something about his expression made me think that the messages had been work related, so I spoke up as he approached. "Work calls, eh, Captain Ward? We've decided to call it an evening. I'm headed back to retirement, Bobby's headed for the Press, and Stan has got nobody to buy him drinks—unless you're staying."

Jim frowned. "Well, if you're the university's detective like the provost says you are, you're not headed back to retirement. I'll see you tomorrow at the crime scene."

He turned to Bobby. "Ms. Slater, there's no need for you to try and go back to work this evening—we've shut down the Press and won't let anybody in until forensics is finished." Jim swallowed. "And you might think about calling a lawyer. It seems you've been heard saying that someone else on campus needs killing—and somebody has done just that."

KEEP READING FOR A PREVIEW OF
HE NEEDED KILLING TOO
BOOK 2 IN THE NEEDED KILLING SERIES

MONDAY MORNING

Jim Ward was sitting on my screen porch and drinking my coffee while he looked at the pages Frank had given me.

"Tell me again why we're meeting here?"

"Because your coffee is better."

I nodded. He was right. My coffee was better but his office equipment was much better than mine. I'd gone out to the drugstore to make photocopies so that we both would have a copy to look at.

"Yeah, but you've got photocopiers and all that other office equipment at the police station."

Jim looked at me. "So buy a photocopier. What are you spending all of the university's money on if not equipment?"

"Well, it looked like I was going to be spending it on coffee beans and half-and-half."

Jim sat back in his chair holding his coffee cup in both hands. "You need to take this seriously, Crawford. If you want to do it.

"Have you settled on a daily rate with Victoria? Have you even checked on how you get a license to be a private detective in this state?"

"I've been thinking about getting business cards."

Ward snorted and shook his head. "Business cards. That's funny. You remember that what you are doing can be dangerous, don't you? People who start resorting to murder as a solution to their problems have a tendency to keep on using that as a solution to other problems—like somebody trying to convict them of murder."

"Now, Jim." I tried to protest.

"Don't 'now, Jim' me, Crawford. Hunting people is a dangerous business and I'll be damned if you'll act like it isn't. Hell, enforcing traffic laws can get a cop killed! How much more dangerous is a known murderer?"

I stopped myself from pointing out that this was an unknown murderer—that being the problem. He was right. Heck, part of the reason I was doing this was the feeling of excitement I'd gotten when I'd closed in on the truth about Sean Thomas's death—murder, that is.

"There is no private investigator licensing for the state of Alabama although a state business license is required to operate any business. Certain cities like Mobile and Birmingham have their own licensing requirements." I hoped it sounded like I was quoting.

"Certain cities including Shelbyville." Jim stared at me. "Get your damn license and then you can meet me at the police station. Until then I'm drinking your damn coffee and you can pay for your own stupid photocopies. OK?"

"Right."

After a pause we went back to the three suspects that Frank had identified—Joyce Fines, Calvin Beck, and Bernard Charles.

I had read the descriptions over the weekend, but Jim was going over them for the first time. I followed along in my copy while Jim read his.

According to the brief biography Frank had included, Joyce Fines was a wildlife ecologist here at the university—a professor emerita. The press had published her first popular book—meaning the first one she'd written for the general public—twenty-five years ago. It had sold slowly but steadily ever since then and was considered to be one of the Press's successes.

Joyce had contacted the Press about updating and releasing a new version. After some back and forth, Philip had flatly rejected the project and had gone so far as to drop the original book from the catalog. Frank noted that it had been the prior press director that had published the book. Philip didn't like being reminded of what his predecessor had done. He told Fines that he didn't like the book and didn't think much of her as an author. She had lost her temper with Philip and suggested that it was people like him who gave snakes a bad reputation. She told him that he was toxic waste and didn't deserve to be breathing.

"Toxic waste?" Ward raised his eyebrows questioningly.

"Bobby says that pond scum has a place in nature, in the environment, but not toxic waste."

"Hmmm." Ward didn't look convinced. "You figure being told you're a lousy writer is grounds to kill a man?"

"Beats me. I've never written a book."

Ward scratched his chin. He seemed to be having a little trouble buying Joyce's motivation. Finally he shrugged. "People get killed for some damn strange reasons. I guess that's one of the strangest I've heard of. What about the next guy?"

The next guy was Calvin Beck—a published nonfiction writer and an aspiring novelist. He had published a number of articles and short stories of the "hook and bullet" genre and was now trying to graduate to full-length novels. He'd submitted his novel directly to Philip. Philip then proceeded to slash the manuscript to pieces and demand extensive changes. Calvin had done all that Philip asked and resubmitted the novel. At that point Philip refused the novel because the author had made all the changes he had suggested.

"Huh?" said Ward. He looked up from the page. "After the author had done what he told him to do?"

"Yeah, Bobby said the guy needed killing."

Frank had gone on to explain that Philip had decided that authors who accept all the changes editors suggest lack the necessary "backbone" to defend their work—a lack of passion. He felt that if Calvin had gone out on a book tour to promote his own book he'd have ended up apologizing for it. Calvin had shown plenty of "passion" at that point. He'd cussed Philip out "down-one-side-and-up-the-other" and, before storming out of the building, had promised to "see Philip in hell even if he had to go there himself."

"Got to say I'd have been mighty angry at that line of reasoning." Jim tapped the page with his forefinger.

"It might interest you to know that 'hook and bullet' means that he writes about fishing and hunting." I'd had to ask Bobby but didn't see any reason to mention that to Jim. "And Bobby said he was more bullet than hook. Didn't write that much about fishing."

"Might not mean much, but I guess knowing which end of a rifle is which is evidence of a sort." He picked up the third sheet of paper. "Did you save the best for last?"

Actually I hadn't even thought to do that. They were still in the order that Frank had given them to me. "See what you think."

For his third suspect, Frank had picked Bernard Charles, the son of Adele Morgan Charles. She was deceased but she had been a famous chronicler of the civil rights movement particularly in Alabama and on this campus. She had written a series of books about her and her colleagues' experiences—none of which were particularly flattering to the state or its institutions of higher education. No one had ever challenged the veracity of what she had written but lots of people hadn't appreciated being written about. Philip's predecessor had decided to publish her works and had upset a number of people in the state.

"You ever read anything she wrote?" Jim stopped to look across the table at me—his finger holding his place on the page.

I shook my head. "Don't think so. Did you?"

"If you had, you'd remember it. People in the black community say she got it right—dead solid right. Pretty impressive for a white woman from Detroit." He dropped his eyes back to the page.

Bernard wanted the Press to reissue those books and publish them as a collection with her last book that she had started but that he had finished after her death. A book in which she traced what had happened in the movement in the following decades.

"Bet some people would be happy if that book never saw the light of day." Jim was so quiet it almost seemed like he was talking to himself.

Philip had no intention of publishing anything that was potentially controversial, not to mention reissuing books that had been controversial. The press held the copyrights and he swore that "as long as he was director" those books would never be reprinted.

Frank went on to note that Bernard had kept his temper and had refrained from saying anything more than, "At least now I know what to do. My mother's books will be reissued. I'll see to that."

"Frank appears to have interpreted that as a death threat."

"So would the district attorney." Jim was staring at the sheets of paper. "And this guy was like this with everybody? Almost seems a shame to try to find out who the murderer was.

"Any more coffee?"

I pushed the thermos over to him.

"I don't know, Crawford. Like I say, murder is either personal or random and this one doesn't feel like there's any randomness to it at all.

"Still we've eliminated most of the Press employees. With the exception of Fulmer and Manning they all have multiple witnesses that clear them. Those two have just got each other to vouch for their whereabouts."

I started to speak and he waved me off. "Oh, I know you are sure they were both blowing smoke at the time, but it doesn't take that long to smoke a joint. They could have come back."

"You seriously believe that they got stoned on marijuana, came back to the Press, shot their boss, and then went home? Is the police department using Reefer Madness as a training film? Hell, the worst thing that probably happened was they got the munchies."

Jim grinned sheepishly and shrugged his shoulders. "OK. So it's weak."

"What about Hazel Murphy? Did she tell you what she refused to tell Harry?"

"I haven't had a chance to interrogate her. She's coming in this afternoon."

"So what do we do next? You want to call these three in? Or wait until you've eliminated all the employees."

Jim sat back in his chair, his coffee cup cradled in his huge hands. "I'm thinking that's just what your provost doesn't want the police doing. He's thinking you'd do it quieter, lower profile, kid gloves, that kind of thing.

"Oh, don't get me wrong. I'll start the routine background checks on all three. We'll find out if any one of them has a history of anger management issues."

"Yeah," I had to agree but it seemed like a strange way to progress. Still, what did I know? This was only my second murder investigation.

"No looking at video in this case, Crawford. This is one where you need to go out and ask questions. Get some answers. See if you can spot the lies because, I'm telling you, everybody lies to the police and they'll lie to you too."

ACKNOWLEDGMENTS

Writing books, I have discovered, is a collaborative effort. At least it is for me. So . . . thanks are due the following people and pets: to everyone who encouraged me along the way (you know who you are); to Hawk, who is muse and model; to Amos, who says he would be less of a nuisance if he could just live on the screen porch; and to Tucker, who believes that being beautiful is enough.

Thanks to Wayne and Anita, who read the whole manuscript in two of its incarnations; to Whit for writerly suggestions; to Jill for advice about police procedures and more; to my neighbor Donna for her encouragement and to Donna in Clarksville for her objective critique and excellent tag words; to Ed, who subbed for JoLee; to Ann for her keen eye; to Van for his enthusiastic support; to Tom, who pointed out typos; to Ruth, who will see her imprint on the book from the opening page; to PJ for help with the blurbs; to Carolyn, Leigh, and Katie for their support. And to Eva (pronounced, so she said, Evah, "as in whatev-ah"), a waitress in the Florida Keys who wanted to be in my book sight unseen, here you are.

Thanks also to my former coworkers for the headset and to Pandora for the music.

ABOUT THE AUTHOR

Writers do not create their works in a vacuum. Or so I believe. They are influenced, sometimes consciously, often unconsciously, by the world around them—by the people they know, the movies and TV shows they watch, the plays and concerts they attend, and, of course, by the books they read.

From the Hardy Boys and Nancy Drew to Perry Mason and Nero Wolfe, I was raised on a steady diet of detective stories. Later, I added to my reading list such authors as Dorothy Sayers, Dick Francis, and Robert B. Parker. They and other writers helped shape my understanding of how to construct a mystery and fueled my love of a good whodunit. Authors outside the genre, notably Robert A. Heinlein, kindled my imagination as a young reader and engendered in me a love of reading that continues to this day. I thank them all for the many wonderful hours I have spent in cloud-cuckoo-land, from the English countryside to the streets of Boston to the far reaches of outer space.

I also owe an odd kind of thank you to the tornado that swept across parts of the South, including Tuscaloosa, Ala., on April 27, 2011. My wife and I came through the tornado physically unharmed, but our lives were changed forever. Like others who have survived an event of such enormity, we began to assess our needs and wants, our hopes and dreams from the perspective of survivors—with the visceral understanding that life is short and the future uncertain.

As a result, I retired from the University of Alabama in September 2011 and took up writing mysteries. I am having a wonderful time, and I hope you enjoy reading my books as much as I enjoy writing them. It's too late for me to keep the day job.

VISIT BILL'S WEBSITE AT BILLFITTSAUTHOR.COM
FOR RECIPES, TESTIMONIALS, AND INFORMATION
ABOUT HOW TO ORDER PAPERBACKS AND EBOOKS
IN THE NEEDED KILLING SERIES.

CPSIA information can be obtained
at www.ICGtesting.com
Printed in the USA
FFOW01n0156220418
46300213-47826FF